CHASE ME,
CATCH NOBODY!

CHASE ME, CATCH NOBODY!

Erik Christian Haugaard

Houghton Mifflin Company Boston

Library of Congress Cataloging in Publication Data

Haugaard, Erik Christian.
  Chase me, catch nobody!

  SUMMARY: On a school trip to Germany in 1937 a
14-year-old Danish schoolboy becomes involved in the
activities of the anti-Nazi underground.
  [1. Germany – History – 1933-1945 – Fiction]
I. Title.
PZ7.H286Ch   [Fic]   80-371
ISBN 0-395-29208-5

For my nieces and nephews, in alphabetical order:
André, Christina, David, Julian, Lisa, Paul, and Peer.

Contents

CHASE ME,
CATCH NOBODY!

1 The Beginning

It all started with the man in the shabby gray raincoat. I am trying to remember his face, but I cannot. Was he a Dane like myself? I am not sure. He spoke Danish; but was it not with an accent?

I shall never know anything about him beyond what I can recall; and that is like a fragment, what you remember of a dream as you are waking up. In any case, what I have just written is not true—it all started earlier. I met the man in the gray raincoat on the ferry sailing to Warnemünde in 1937. But why was I on board, why was I traveling to Germany?

In 1937 I was fourteen years old, a schoolboy still. I was blond, blue-eyed, of medium height, and squarely built; in other words, a perfectly ordinary Danish boy. My appearance at that time was a source of disappointment to me. I had begun to imagine that I might become a poet, and the snub-nosed image which looked back at me from the mirror did not please me.

I was an only child. My parents were then well-to-do. They, too, failed to live up to my expectations. Even now I blush at the thought of the sources from which our wealth was derived. My father was a wholesaler who imported various commodities into Denmark, the most important item being licorice-allsorts. When I was younger, I had been inclined to consider it the best business anyone could be engaged in.

Not only was my father's means of earning a living hard to contemplate without a shudder by a young poet, but so was the man himself. In my youth I judged my parents harshly. My father was the kind of person who lived for today, giving as little thought to tomorrow as that distant date deserved. He was fond of his wife and dressed her well, fond of his child and gave him too large a weekly allowance; but he was fondest of all of his motorcar. He loved parties, a drink before dinner, and friends—without ever wondering why they were his friends. As soon as he had become an adult, he had given up all the childish follies he had been forced to pursue in school, such as reading books.

With their usual lack of imagination, my parents had baptized me Erik. There were four Eriks in my class. My last name was not, and is not, an illustrious one; it is Hansen, which means "son of Hans," the commonest name in Denmark.

As you can guess from the little I have said, I was—if the truth must be told, and it always should be in a book —a bit of a snob.

2

I am also telling you all this because, since I can recall nothing of the man in the gray raincoat, it is of importance that you should know something about the boy who met him. But why was I on the ferry? That too will have to be explained before the story can properly begin.

About a month earlier, in my German class, I had received a duplicated letter for my parents, in which they were informed that a trip to Lübeck and Hamburg was planned for children from our own and another school. There was further information about cost, times of departure and return, as well as an admonition not to give any participant too large a sum for pocket money. This week-long excursion was to take place during the Easter holidays. I had no particular wish to go for two good reasons: first, none of my friends would be going; and second, I considered the teacher in charge my enemy. What he considered me, I never gave a thought.

I delivered the note during dinner. My father glanced at it, but made no comments. These came later in the evening and I was not meant to hear them.

I had been reading in bed. Before I turned off the light I wanted a glass of milk and possibly a cookie or two if there were any left in the jar in the kitchen. As I was making my way downstairs, I heard my father and mother talking in the living room, and they mentioned my name.

"If Erik goes with the school to Germany for Easter, we could motor up to Oslo." My father's voice was happy; obviously he was looking forward to the trip to Oslo. I could not make out my mother's reply, but it could not have been negative, for my father answered with a laugh. "It will do him good—they will teach him a bit of discipline there. The trouble is we spoil him."

I wanted to protest, but if you are eavesdropping you can't. This time I did hear my mother. "He is at a difficult age." I could not hear her sigh but I am sure she did, before she added, "Vacations can be very trying."

What else was said I did not hear. In fury I returned to my room, without even going to the kitchen, and jumped right back into bed.

Somehow the idea that parents as positively awful as mine should find me "trying" was unbearable. It took me a long time to fall asleep, and I contemplated several different forms of revenge before my eyes closed.

The next day I decided that since my parents did not love me, which was obvious, the most dignified posture which I could assume was one of cold indifference to them. When you are boiling with rage inside, this is a most difficult part to play. At breakfast, I insisted that I wanted to go on that trip to Germany, which I didn't want to take; and a week later, when my father told me of his and my mother's plan to travel to Norway, I managed to look interested rather than disappointed and hurt.

As Easter drew nearer, I learned that only twenty boys from my school were going to Germany, and from my own class no more than three besides myself. Two of the boys I distinctly disliked; the third was not an enemy but not a friend either. As for the teacher in charge, he taught history and gymnastics: physical education . . . pushups! He was tall and straight, with those water-blue eyes that remind you not so much of the sky as of the void of the universe. He liked to start every physical education class with an edifying little speech, wherein

4

such maxims as "a healthy mind in a healthy body" were liberally sprayed over our heads. I never minded these little pep talks, for to tell you the truth there is no nonsense so silly that I would not rather listen to it than do pushups or "slow twisting of the torso, with rotating arms and gyrating toes."

It is only fair, right in the beginning of a book, to warn your reader of your prejudices. Among mine is, was, and always will be, a strong dislike of physical education. I suspect that those who worship the body have contempt for the mind. The two must never be equated, it is "the mortal frame" and the "immortal soul." Now, do not think for a moment that I was a little weakling, who secretly envied the athlete. No, as a matter of fact, I was rather strongly built and my vision was perfect. Nor was I a brilliant scholar. I was nearer to the bottom of the class than to the top. I was never one of those boys whose hand shot up in the air only seconds after a teacher had asked a question. I belonged among those who ducked their heads in order to appear as small as possible, and whose constant prayer was, "Oh God, make me invisible until the bell rings and the lesson is over."

And what does this have to do with the man in the gray raincoat? Very little and yet a lot, for if I had not been the kind of boy I was, I might have refused the package which he asked me to carry through the customs. Life is a jigsaw puzzle; each little jagged piece fits somewhere, and therefore they are all of importance.

The night before my departure for Germany, my mother had a talk with me. She had packed my suitcase first: seven pairs of underwear, seven pairs of socks, four shirts, one sweater, all of it carefully folded. Have I forgotten to mention the pajamas and the handkerchiefs? Well, there were six of the latter, and the former were striped, red and blue.

"Erik, don't mess up the shirts. They are on the bottom; take them out one by one."

"Yes, Mother," I answered. I was already in bed.

My mother sat down beside me. "Neatness is not a sin," she said with a sigh, and then contemplating my head she added, "You could do with a haircut."

I merely made a grimace; next to teachers of physical exercises I have always disliked barbers most.

"Long hair gets tangled and is dirty-looking. In Germany you will find everyone wearing their hair short." It is amazing how adept parents can be at saying the wrong thing. "Your father has his hair trimmed twice a month."

"Yes, Mother." I closed my eyes pretending to be falling asleep.

"Has your father talked to you?" The way my mother pronounced the words made me wide awake.

"No," I replied with my most angelic smile.

"He promised to." My mother frowned. "After all, you are almost a grownup. I mean a big boy."

I muttered yes, and looked inquiringly at her. She in embarrassment turned her head away. "I mean about men and women." My mother blushed and for a moment she looked like a young girl. "Your father ought to talk to you about it."

Feeling sorry for my mother I said quickly, "Oh, I know all about that."

6

"Do you really?" My mother felt relieved—I could hear that in the tone of her voice—and for a moment, remembering the many battles I had fought and lost over the length of my hair, I wished I had not said anything.

"You see, I wanted your father to talk to you, because you will be alone. I mean we won't be there and you might get into bad company."

I thought of the teacher who was to be one of the leaders of the group, and silently agreed with my mother that I certainly ran a fair chance of finding myself in bad company.

"Promise to stay with your teacher, and . . . and . . ." My mother looked around the room as if she were liable to find the words which had escaped her in some corner of it.

"Be a good boy," I finished the sentence for her.

"That wasn't what I was going to say." She laughed and let her hand glide through my hair. "My big boy," she said and smiled and for that moment, in that little space of time, we loved each other as a mother and son should. But I knew it wouldn't last and so did she; yet I think we both enjoyed it, for neither of us spoke for some time, as if we knew that when we did we would destroy that intimacy.

"Father will drive you to the station in the morning." My mother rose and walked to the door. There she turned and wished me good-night.

I reached up and turned off my bed lamp. I have always thought those last moments before you fall asleep the most precious of the day. Comfortably warm, you can lie there and think about everything that has happened

7

to you that day, reliving certain moments of it, until the shadows in your room grow black and you fall asleep.

I touched the place in my bed where my mother had been sitting; it was still warm. I smiled, for I had noticed that my mother had seen that my clothes were thrown across a chair, my trousers all wrinkled, as she wished me good-night. She had said nothing, and that had been kind of her.

'I will try to be more orderly,' I promised myself, feeling as virtuous as if I had already managed to become it.

The moon was shining in through the window and its light reflected in the glass wall of my aquarium. I could just make out the shadow of a fish moving. 'I must remember to feed them in the morning,' I thought, and then I fell asleep.

"Mother asked me to talk to you." As my father changed gears he threw me a quick glance and a comradely smile meant to disarm me. I merely said yes and looked out the window; we were passing the bakery where in the summer they sold homemade ice cream and cones.

"Damn it all. I mean, you must know all about it." My father's face was flushed and I could not help feeling sorry for him. "Don't they teach you something about it in school?"

"Yes," I laughed, "but not before next year."

"Then, if you don't know, you will have to wait until next year to find out." My father grinned. "I never thought it would be so difficult to talk about; after all, I am not shy . . . It is all very natural if you love one an-other."

That was exactly my trouble, I did know all about sex, but as to finding it natural . . . No, I thought it all rather repulsive. I would never have admitted this to anyone, least of all to my father, so I said yes as I imagined a man of the world would have said it.

I must have succeeded far beyond expectations, for my father asked if I had ever loved a girl. He said this in such a way that I was left in no doubt of what he meant, and now I blushed. At first I was going to answer yes, but then I thought a lie would be even more childish than having to admit that I had never as much as kissed a girl.

"Don't be in a hurry, Erik." My father's voice was kind. "Innocence is no sin."

I thought of certain of my classmates, especially one who was always taunting me. It might not be a sin but it was something almost worse—it left you open to ridicule. "I have never met any girl I cared for," I said, while with relief I saw that we were near the station.

"Not even Kirsten?" my father teased.

"She is ugly!" I exclaimed with such emphasis that it embarrassed me, for it was not true and I was fonder of that girl than any other I knew. Though I should add that I did not know many, attending as I did an all-boys school.

My father laughed but said nothing more, for which I was thankful. If he had I might have burst out crying, which would have been mortifying. How can one ex-

9

plain that your tongue so often says the very opposite of what you mean? It is as if there were an inborn traitor, a turncoat and weathercock ready at any time to claim possession of you.

"I will just see you to your train." My father had parked the car outside the station. "How much money did Mother give you?"

"Thirty crowns," I answered. I knew that in the letter to the parents, the teachers in charge of the trip had asked that the maximum pocket money should not exceed twenty-five.

"Here . . ." My father took out his wallet and gave me two ten-crown bills. "It might come in handy." Then before I could object he gave my shoulder a slight, affectionate shove and each of us opened a door and got out. It would be easy to say that my father wanted to buy his son's affection, but it would not be true. He loved giving money away; his generosity gave him pleasure.

As we entered the great hall of the main railroad station in Copenhagen, my father stopped to look at a poster. It was a colorful photograph of a German village surrounded by snowcapped mountains; in the foreground peasants were dancing in national costumes. Across the top of the poster it said VISIT BAVARIA and at the bottom was the insignia of the German State Railways.

My father shook his head. "Erik," he began, "I am not interested in politics, you know that."

I nodded, while I looked around to see if anyone from my school had arrived.

"But if I were you, I wouldn't believe too much in that." My father pointed towards the spot on the poster where the swastika was. Then suddenly he grinned. "You know, my boy, the bigger the package of chocolate, the more paper there is in it. Well, it is the same with Germany."

At the other end of the hall, I had spied the figure of the teacher from my school surrounded by a group of boys. "There they are!" I shouted.

"Indeed." My father smiled toward the children as if they were near enough to distinguish his friendly grimace. "I suppose I should say hello to your teacher?" he mumbled.

"You don't have to," I answered. Just then a boy walked by with a knapsack on his back. Kurt Madsen was from my class in school and I did not like him. But he greeted me by name, and I introduced him to my father.

"Well, you run along with your friend." My father's relief at not having to accompany me any further was all too apparent. I shook hands with him and Kurt bowed as if we were in dancing school and he had just invited my father to be his partner in a polka.

As we walked toward the group of boys, I looked back at my father. At that very moment he turned and waved. I raised my hand and smiled, knowing that that self-same smile would be on my father's face; and it occurred to me that my father and I had the same faults, which was why we didn't get along.

11

2 The Man in the Gray Raincoat

"It has always struck me, every time I see this building, that thus the great halls of the Viking kings must have looked." The teacher lifted his arm toward the ceiling of the station. "Don't you think so, boys?" Some of the pupils near me made grunts of approval as if they, too, always had such thoughts. I followed the direction of his hand. The roof of the central station in Copenhagen is rather impressive, being constructed from great beams of wood.

"We will have roll call, to see if everyone is here," a small fat man declared and then added with a jolly laugh, "It wouldn't do to lose anyone before we start."

The roll call revealed that we were all there, bar one. A boy called Nikolai Linde was missing. "Fifty-two, the number of cards in a deck." The fat man, who was a teacher from the other Copenhagen school, laughed again. "Mr. Nikolai is the knave of spades."

I sat down on my suitcase. All of the other boys had knapsacks, some with little Danish flags attached to them. "He is an idiot," I whispered to Kurt. He nodded, but not as if he meant it, and I thought to myself, 'And you are another one!' The whole trip seemed to be getting off to a fine start: two idiot teachers for leaders and fifty-two idiots as followers. I grinned and corrected myself, fifty-one, just as the knave of spades appeared.

Nikolai Linde was accompanied by his mother, a large woman with a commanding voice. She introduced herself and her son to the two teachers. Nikolai bowed first to them and then to his mother, who kissed him on the cheek and told him to be a good boy and mind the grownups.

The poor fellow looked as if he were too used to such behavior on his mother's part to be embarrassed by it. Some of the other boys laughed; but I sympathized with Nikolai; he, too, was carrying a suitcase, though it was not a leather one like mine.

"Line up by twos," the tall teacher from my school ordered. His name was Mr. Nielson. The *son* instead of the usual Danish *sen* was by courtesy of a paternal Swedish grandfather. The *mister* sounded wrong, somehow. It should have been Herr Nielson. *Herr* means "master," and certainly, *Mister* Nielson thought himself a master.

On principle I always fall in last in such processions and I make a point of being out of step—it is not much of a protest. The fat teacher came at the tail end, holding a large suitcase with a broken lock that had forced him to tie a rope around it.

Though I had no friends among the boys from my

13

own school I stuck with them. We were eight in the compartment: the four from my class, three from the one above ours, whom I only knew by sight, and then, strangely enough, Nikolai Linde. He did not go to our school and we were rather surprised to find him among us.

There had been a fight for the window seats, which neither Nikolai nor I had taken part in. I chose one of the places farthest away from the window. I knew I should be able to keep that; besides, they are the most comfortable seats because you have a corner to lean against and it is easy for you to retreat to the corridor if the company in the compartment becomes unbearable. Nikolai had sat down beside me and when I looked at him he smiled back.

The train started with such a lurch that a suitcase in the rack above the seats fell down. No one was hurt. The suitcase was Nikolai's, and he picked it up as if he were in no way surprised that such a thing should befall him. One of the older boys who had gotten a window seat shoved it back up, grumbling while he did it. Nikolai thanked him profusely and declared loudly how pleased he was that no one had been hurt. Since the only head that had been in any real danger was his own, this seemed to be rather overdoing it.

"The teacher, the fat one, is he from your school?" I asked.

Nikolai grinned. "He teaches German and geography, and he is called Stinker Larsen."

"Why, does he smell?" Nearly every teacher in my

school had a nickname that more or less aptly described him.

"No, but he claims we do. Even in winter he has to have a window open. He says he is allergic to the smell of small repulsive boys. He is all right, though." Nikolai nodded to emphasize his last statement. "That tall one must be one of yours."

"He is commonly known as the Lighthouse, and he teaches gymnastics and history. He likes boys with short hair and straight backs, and he hates longhaired, spine-less loafers."

Nikolai touched his own hair, which was very short, and then remarked with a sigh, "He would get along with my mother."

"He is an awful ass," I said. "But if you know how, you can handle him." I was going to explain what I meant, but just at that moment the Lighthouse opened the door to our compartment.

"Our carriage is not being taken aboard the ferry. When we arrive at Gedser, I want you all to fall in by twos on the platform. We shall march on board." The Lighthouse paused and looked around at us as if he were expecting us to question his order. Two of the older boys and Kurt said, "Yes," in audible tones; the rest of us either said nothing or mumbled in agreement.

"We could sing a song as we marched on board."

I almost gasped. Nikolai's voice sounded as if he really meant it. I turned to stare at him in wonder. He was looking at the Lighthouse with the most submissive of servile expressions on his face.

15

The teacher flushed. You could see that he was debating with himself whether or not he was being made a fool of. At last Nikolai's humble smile convinced him that he was not. "That would be nice, but I am afraid that there are those who might not want to join in." The Lighthouse looked in my direction. "Or who possibly might not know any songs."

"What a pity!" Nikolai sounded genuinely sorry.

"But that doesn't mean we can't get on board the ship a bit more smartly than we got on the train." The Lighthouse was now staring straight at me.

"We are not in the army, sir," I blurted out, forgetting my first and most important resolution, 'Don't ever affront a teacher if you can avoid it.'

"Erik Hansen." The Lighthouse's voice was as sharp as a drill sergeant's.

"Yes, sir," I answered, trying not to look the least bit scared.

"I was surprised to find your name on the list of boys going to Germany, and if you don't know how to behave, I will have you sent back on the next train."

"Yes, sir," I mumbled, wishing I were on it already.

"I intend to keep an eye on you," he warned as he closed the door.

"Damn you!" I swore and dug an elbow into Nikolai's side. "That was all your fault."

"Ouch!" Nikolai grimaced. "I couldn't help it. He is a worse fool than Stinker Larsen." Nikolai jumped up and, standing by the door, he parodied the Lighthouse giving his little speech about us marching on board. Some of the boys laughed; but to my surprise, Kurt and

16

an older boy, the one who had thrown Nikolai's suitcase back into the rack, looked annoyed.

We didn't sing, and we walked rather than marched on board, though like the animals embarking on Noah's Ark, we proceeded two by two. The Lighthouse stood by the gangway. As Nikolai and I walked past, he smiled sarcastically. To make certain that the teacher would never forgive nor forget us, Nikolai said in the loudest of stage whispers, "Shouldn't we salute?"

The ferry was an old one, from the turn of the century, with two tall, thin funnels. Inside, all of the wood was mahogany and there was plenty of polished brasswork. I was eager to inspect the ship and had no particular desire for the companionship of Nikolai, but he was as hard to get rid of as a flea.

Through an open hatch we could see down into the engine room. The smell of steam and coal was pleasant, at least I found it so, and turning to Nikolai I said, "I would love to be the captain of such a ship."

"I wouldn't," he answered, still peering down into the engine room. "My father is a stoker." With a nod towards the bowels of the ship, he added, "It is hot down there, especially if you are sailing in the tropics."

Nikolai was several inches shorter than I was, so if I said at that moment I looked up to him it would hardly be correct, for as a matter of mere physical fact, I looked down on him when I asked, "Does your father sail in the tropics?"

"The China run." Nikolai sounded bored.

"A stoker on the China run," I repeated, while inwardly I cursed my father for having chosen to be something as unromantic as a wholesaler.

"He is a grease monkey on a diesel ship now, but he used to be a stoker on the America Line." Nikolai looked back towards the harbor of Gedser. "My father is a Communist—what is yours?"

"A Liberal, I guess," I said, though I felt far from certain which party my father voted for.

"Personally, I think I am going to be an anarchist," said Nikolai very seriously as we climbed the companionway to the upper deck.

I didn't know what an anarchist was. The only definition of it that I had ever seen had been in a cartoon, a humorous picture of a wild bearded man standing on a soapbox screaming, "PULL EVERYTHING DOWN!" To which a smaller man in the drawing had answered, "EXCEPT FOR CARROTS AND RADISHES; THEY HAVE TO BE PULLED UP!"

"I am not very political," I mumbled. I was watching the gulls that swarmed by the hundreds around the ship.

"Where we are going, it is all fascist." Nikolai nodded towards the bow of the ship and Germany beyond it.

"They are Nazis," I corrected.

"Nazis or fascists, it is all the same." Nikolai frowned. "I want to see it."

"Well, you are going to." One of the gulls seemed to have hurt its wing and was flying awkwardly. The other gulls were attacking the injured bird, swooping down at it again and again.

"They are just like human beings," someone said. A small, thin man wearing a shabby gray raincoat was standing right behind us. "Watch them!" he exclaimed. The gulls had managed to force their wounded comrade down upon the water and were now pecking at it.

"Like *some* human beings," I corrected. I thought it was too easy to say we were all like the gulls.

The stranger laughed—a sour, joyless laugh. "Wait, my boy, and you shall be wiser. Where we are going they are worse than those." With his hand he made a sweep upward toward the screaming gulls. Then, as if he regretted having spoken to us at all, he made a funny little bow, turned on his heel and walked down the companionway.

"He was a queer creature." I looked at Nikolai. "I mean, what he said about the gulls."

"He may have been a schoolteacher." Nikolai smirked. "Stinker Larsen always says that anyone who has taught school longer than one year knows two things: first, that Darwin was right, the average little Danish boy has not *as*cended but *de*scended from the apes; and secondly, that humanity is a genetic catastrophe."

I grinned and looked back. The wake of the ferry made a slight curve; we must be changing course. I could no longer see the wounded gull. I wondered who the man was; a schoolteacher I was sure he was not. I couldn't recall what he had looked like at all and I asked Nikolai if he could.

"He had a raincoat on, a gray one. It was frayed at the collar, I think." Nikolai wrinkled his brow in an effort to remember more, then with a shrug of his shoulder he gave up. "He was the flying Dutchman, he has taken over the ship and we shall never get to Warnemünde."

I laughed, but said, "You are right in a way, he was

19

like someone you see in a dream. While you are sleeping they are so real to you, but when you wake up, they fade away and become shadows."

"A seagoing ghost," Nikolai said in a hollow voice. "Look." He pointed aft. "Denmark is disappearing."

A slight mist was obscuring the coastline. As we watched the land merged with the sky and the sea, and was gone. I shivered; it was cold here on the upper deck. "Let's go down below," I suggested.

3 The Package

In the saloon, we found the other boys sitting around tables, eating their sandwiches. The dining room was farther aft. Here only tea, coffee, beer, and soft drinks were sold. In the school's letter to the parents, it had been recommended that we bring sandwiches for the first meal of our journey.

Nikolai and I sat down at a table and nodded to the four boys who were already there—I did not know any of them. When the waiter came, I ordered a grape tonic; but Nikolai pretended not to notice him, while he drew from his own pocket a very flat little package.

My sandwiches were in a bag; each one had been carefully wrapped in greaseproof paper by our maid. Danish open sandwiches can be about the best food you can eat. The first one I undid was roast beef with lots of fried onions on top. Nikolai's tiny packet was on the table before him: four slices of black bread, with salami cut so

21

thin that if there had been any wind it might have blown away. Nikolai eyed my roast beef, and I his salami; then, he lowered his eyes.

"Should we swap?" I suggested, blushing. It is not difficult to be generous but it is embarrassing.

Nikolai looked at my roast beef sandwich, then at the bag it had come out of, and decided that I would not suffer undue hardship by being deprived of it. "Sure," he agreed, and offered me a choice of one of four identical and equally sad-looking salami sandwiches.

When the waiter brought me my grape tonic I asked Nikolai if he didn't want something to drink, adding that I had plenty of money. The boy looked at me with a wry smile and then asked me whether we were friends.

"Sure," I said and I meant it, for I had taken a great liking to him.

Nikolai ordered an orange squash; and as soon as the waiter was gone he whispered so the other boys at the table could not hear him: "I have only five crowns for the whole trip, so I have to be careful . . . You see, I earned the money myself to pay for it."

The bread underneath the salami had been spread with margarine. I ate it quickly, wondering what else was in my bag.

I had hoped that the rest of my sandwiches would be plainer. But I should have known that my mother would never let me down, especially when there was a chance of showing off. There was duck with apple and prunes, left over from Friday night's dinner; then roast pork with crackling and red cabbage; and, as the chief attraction, a slice of white bread liberally covered with smoked salmon.

It was while I was eating this last sandwich that the Lighthouse came over to honor us with his presence. He eyed my smoked salmon with a look almost as hungry as Nikolai had given my roast beef.

As far as I was concerned, Danish schoolteachers were overpaid; but I am afraid that the Lighthouse would not have agreed with me on that point. Certainly, he could not afford to eat smoked salmon.

"I hate to interrupt an orgy." The Lighthouse was not looking at me but at my sandwich. "Before we disembark, you are all to line up at the gangway on the port side." With a bitter smile, undoubtedly recalling his own lunch, he said to me, "You do yourself well."

I cursed my mother, but I cursed the Lighthouse even more. There was nothing to be done; he would be on my back for the whole trip.

"It is a bit too fatty and heavy, sir, after duck," I commented before I swallowed the last bite. "I have never become King, but I do live royally, sir." I wiped my hands on the bag my sandwiches had been in and emptied my glass of soda water without looking up at the Lighthouse.

Nikolai swore that the teacher's face was as red as a Danish flag and that he almost died of a stroke. Personally, I wish he had; even now, the Lighthouse is still one of those people whom it is impossible for me to contemplate while remaining calm.

Later I explained to Nikolai what I had meant when I spoke about never becoming King. The Lighthouse had a little game that he liked us to play once in a while, when he got bored with "disciplining our bodies." It was an extremely simple one, which came naturally to his not overly complex mind. With a piece of chalk, he divided the floor of the gymnasium into five equal areas. He called them "territories." The first was labeled KING, the next PRINCE, the following ARISTOCRAT, the fourth COMMONER, and the last was called SLAVES. Now the whole class was herded into the KING space, and when the whistle blew, a free-for-all took place. The idea was to push, shove, and throttle every other one of your classmates until you alone were in the KING territory. This was repeated until there was only one PRINCE, one ARISTOCRAT, and one COMMONER. All the rest were SLAVES. To show my contempt for this charming contest, I always walked straight down to the SLAVES' quarters as soon as the Lighthouse blew his whistle. "He claims it illustrates Darwin's theory of the 'Survival of the Fittest,'" I exclaimed in fury.

Nikolai looked at me thoughtfully. "He is a fascist . . . a pure fascist."

"A fascist . . ." I repeated. It was a nice-sounding word and I was getting used to it.

"Yes." Nikolai laughed. "That is why he wants us to march everywhere. Fascists love playing soldiers. I wonder how he and Stinker Larsen will get along . . . Look, there is the fellow in the raincoat."

The man who had talked to us on the upper deck was now looking around the saloon as if he were searching for someone. He seemed to be on his way over to Nikolai and me when two men entered the saloon, and then he must have changed his mind, for he made his way rapidly and determinedly towards the nearest door.

24

"They are the police," I said. "He is a jewel thief and they are after him." To my surprise, for I hadn't been serious, the two men left by the same door as he had.

"Why don't they arrest him then?" Nikolai shook his head. "They don't look like police to me."

"And what do the police look like?" I asked, a little annoyed.

"I don't think they are Danes." Nikolai jumped up. "Come on," he urged excitedly, and we rushed out on deck.

The railing was crowded with people. We could see the shore of Germany; we were not far from Warnemünde. Standing a little apart from the others was our friend. The two men, whom Nikolai had not convinced me were not police, were a few feet away from us; they did not seem particularly interested in the view.

"You go over and stand next to him, and I'll try to get as near to the others as I can, without being conspicuous," Nikolai whispered, though there was so much noise that no one else could have heard him had he spoken out loud. "Try and look as natural as you can."

"That shouldn't be difficult. I feel like an idiot already," I replied irritably; for in truth, I did not like the way Nikolai had taken over. Still, I obeyed.

I made my way slowly to the man in the gray raincoat, without glancing directly at him even once, as though he concerned me no more than any of the rest of the passengers. For a few minutes we stood next to each other, both staring at the approaching shore, as if that headland were of absorbing interest. I could now see the white sand of the beach and some large buildings, which I

25

assumed were hotels, for Warnemünde was a summer resort.

"Don't look at me. Go to the men's toilet on the upper deck on the starboard side, near the first-class saloon, and wait there."

I cast a fleeting glance at my companion; he was staring out into space, as if he were not aware of my existence or anyone else's.

As I passed the two men who had been following the man in the gray raincoat, I could not help smiling. Nikolai had engaged them in conversation in his best "school" German. 'It won't be easy for them to shake him off,' I thought, 'he'll stick to them like a burr.'

I went through the large saloon and up the staircase at the rear of it. Now I was on the upper deck; but which side was starboard? I closed my eyes and it came to me: 'Starboard is on your right when you face the bow of the ship.'

There was the sign, plain as could be: HERREN TOILET. I almost turned around and walked away. There was something so hopelessly sordid in such a meeting place. If only he had said, "by the third lifeboat on the upper deck," that would have been romantic. But by the third lifeboat, everyone could have observed us. No, the toilet on the starboard side, near the first-class saloon, was a lot more sensible. With a sigh, I opened the door and stepped inside.

It was empty. The locks on the three toilets all read vacant. I walked over to one of the sinks and started to wash my hands. 'What does that fellow want with me?' I thought. 'Chances are that he is a thief. If I were reason-

26

able, I would go out and find the rest of the boys and forget all about him! But if I did, what would Nikolai say?'

I looked at my face in the mirror above the sink; a snub-nosed boy gazed back at me. I made a grimace and so did he; then I laughed...And then...the door opened and the man in the gray raincoat stepped inside.

I read the question on his face and remarked quickly, "We are alone. There is no one else here."

"Can I trust you?" he asked, but he did not wait for me to answer. "I must... I must..." he muttered, and taking a package from his coat pocket, he thrust it at me. "I will come and get it back from you, as soon as the train is moving and we have passed through customs." His lips turned upwards in a strange, thin little smile, as if he were not used to such expressions. "It is not diamonds," he mumbled. "I am not a thief!"

I wanted to explain to him that I had never thought that he was—although strictly speaking that would not have been the truth.

"Someone is coming," he exclaimed suddenly, and pushed me into one of the empty cubicles. "Stay there until at least five minutes after I am gone."

Confused, I locked the door and stared stupidly at its painted surface. Someone had scratched a dirty limerick on it.

"If you don't see me again, deliver it in Hamburg to the Golden Lamb, in Keblerstrasse. It's in the Altstadt. Say you are a friend of Christian Wahnschaffe."

I heard the door open. He was leaving; but someone else entered at the same time. Was it the two Germans?

27

No one was talking, not even in a whisper. I looked at my watch. How slowly the second hand moved! I read the limerick on the door and the other messages that were scratched on the walls and it struck me that you could use these dirty verses for codes, if you were a spy. But I was not a spy. Or was I? I looked at the package which I still held in my hand. It was a little too big for my trouser pocket; I slid it inside my sweater and buttoned up my jacket. I straightened my tie; then I opened the door.

A man was washing his hands; he did not even look up. I noticed that the package made a bulge. 'All I have to do is throw it overboard, into the sea,' I told myself. But I knew that I wouldn't.

Our baggage was in a corner of the main saloon; if I could get there before the others came, I could manage to put the package in my suitcase.

'You are a fool!' I thought as I hurried down the stairs; but somehow I did not feel like one.

4   And What It Contained

My suitcase was the most stupid place that I could have hid the package, for surely if the customs officials had looked through our luggage, they would have found it; my excuse must be that I was new to smuggling and international intrigues. But none of our rucksacks or suitcases had been as much as opened; we had been rushed through customs without any inspection at all, our youthful faces taken as a guarantee of our innocence.

"You must remember that here in Germany, we are guests." The Lighthouse looked at us searchingly; we were lined up on the platform just before entering the train. "A guest must be courteous to his host, and I expect all of you to behave in a manner that will not dishonor our country."

Nikolai nudged me and I grinned.

"Think of yourselves as ambassadors of Denmark." The Lighthouse's voice rose. "And let the German youth

29

see that we too have awakened to the spirit of our new age."

At the word "awakened," Nikolai had made a loud snoring noise, which earned him laughter from a few of the boys, a smile from Stinker Larsen, and a venomous glance from the Lighthouse.

"You can be glad he is not your teacher—he would kill you when he had you back in the gym," I whispered to Nikolai just as the Lighthouse gave us marching orders.

This was my first trip beyond the borders of Denmark. No, that is not quite true. I had been across the Sound to Sweden, but that is not really a foreign country—at least not to a Dane. Entering a German passenger train would have been exciting in itself; just reading DO NOT LEAN OUT OF THE WINDOW and SPITTING IS FORBIDDEN is somehow adventurous in a strange language. But I had no time for such childishness, for my whole mind was occupied by one thought: What was in the package lying beneath my striped pajamas in my suitcase?

Although all of the passengers semed to have boarded the train, there was no sign that it was about to depart. Nikolai and I had taken seats on either side of the door to the compartment. "Let's go out into the corridor," he suggested. Quickly I glanced up at my suitcase hanging in the net above my seat; it would be quite safe.

"They were Germans, all right," Nikolai said, grinning. I still had not told my friend about the package that the man in the gray raincoat had given me.

"I kept asking them all sorts of silly questions. I am sure they were after our friend because when he walked away, they got desperate. I think if they had dared they'd

30

have tossed me overboard . . . Where did you go and why?"

"Did they notice me?" I asked a little too anxiously. "I mean, did they seem to care when I left?"

Nikolai frowned. "I can't remember, but I don't think so."

We had walked to the end of the corridor and were now standing before the open door of the railroad car. We could see the wharf and the Danish ferry docked alongside it.

"Look!" Nikolai exclaimed.

The man in the gray raincoat was coming down the gangway, but he was not alone; the men who had been watching him on board held him firmly by the arms. As they stepped onto the pier, they were met by three people in uniform. One of the men who was escorting our friend clicked his heels and raised his arm in the Nazi salute. "*Heil* Hitler!" He shouted so loud that we could hear him plainly.

His greeting was returned by one of the uniformed men, in a manner that left no doubt that the latter was a superior returning the salute of an inferior. It was the man in the shabby gray raincoat who interested the officer. We knew that he was speaking to him, but we could not hear what he was saying.

A conductor came in a great rush and closed the door. There was a jerk and the train started. I managed to pull down the window in the door, and leaning out I caught a last glimpse of the man in the gray raincoat. There he stood, a lone figure surrounded by his enemies.

"That was the Gestapo!" Nikolai's voice was as excited

31

as a beetle collector's when he has just discovered a new insect.

"The Gestapo ..." I repeated uncertainly. I knew that they were a kind of police force of Hitler's, without knowing exactly what they did. As I have said, I came from a home in which the weather was discussed with more interest than politics. My parents and their friends would not be aware of the tidal waves of history before they were submerged and drowned under one of them.

"They will torture him." Nikolai nodded in agreement with himself. "They are worse than the S.S."

"Which ones are the police?" I asked, and then blushed, aware that this was a stupid question.

"The *Waffen* S.S. is a collection of criminals of the most common variety—mere brutes. The Gestapo is a more refined instrument. Its members are sadists but not necessarily idiots."

Nikolai lectured me in words that weren't his own. He had learned them by heart. Still I was impressed, for I was so ignorant that even the Spanish Civil War had been no more than a newspaper headline to me. But there were those in my school who took politics more seriously. Several of the boys belonged to the Conservative Youth. Not long ago, before it was forbidden, they had dressed in black uniforms; now they only wore silver badges.

The flat countryside whirled by with such speed that I thought, 'You, Erik, are standing still and the world is rotating in front of you; and if you stand here, staring out of the window long enough, China will come whizzing past.'

At that moment, Nikolai, who had been giving me a

detailed and depressing description of Hitler's rise to power, stopped talking, and someone behind me said, "*Heil* Hitler!"

I turned to face a middle-aged man, who, when I did not respond, looked very perturbed.

"He wants to go to the toilet," Nikolai mumbled, pushing me away from the door.

"I'm sorry," I said in Danish, forgetting that this gentleman would probably not understand me unless I spoke German. As he closed the door behind him, I whispered to Nikolai, "Do they always say *Heil* Hitler before they go to the toilet?"

"*Immer* . . ." Nikolai grinned. "Always . . . Let's go back to our compartment."

Before I sat down in my seat, I glanced up at my suitcase. It lay securely in the net, looking as inconspicuous as it could. Suddenly I recalled what Nikolai had said when we had seen the man in the gray raincoat being marched away by the Gestapo. "They will torture him." Those were his words. To me the idea of torture had something to do with the Middle Ages, with times so long past that only history teachers could remember them. Once, in the castle at Elsinore, I had seen a dungeon so tiny that the prisoner could not even lie down. Yet in spite of the heavy walls, it had not frightened me, for it had not seemed real. Perhaps the absence of toads, snakes, and rats had made the cell so unconvincing.

What would happen if they tortured the man in the gray raincoat? Would he not at the very first sight of the thumbscrews say, "Oh, I gave that package to a young Danish boy with a snub nose"? It was then that I tried to recall his features, because I wanted to examine them in order to judge how well he would stand up under torture; I realized that I couldn't remember what he looked like at all. Only that silly worn-out raincoat had stayed in my mind.

I nodded my head in the direction of the corridor as a sign to Nikolai and got up. As soon as I had closed the door of the compartment behind me I asked, "Are you sure they will torture him?"

"They always do." His tone as well as his words left little possibility of doubt.

"And then do they tell ... I mean ..." I knew I sounded confused.

"They usually crack, but some are brave," Nikolai answered from his vast experience of human depravity.

In my encounters with the school's bullies, I had never covered myself in glory, and I felt very certain that I would "crack." But the man in the gray raincoat may have been made of sterner stuff. I was just about to tell Nikolai about the package when the train started to slow down. We were coming into the station at Lübeck.

"The Youth Hostel where we are staying is about a ten-minute walk from here. Please stay together. I wouldn't miss any of you if you got lost, but there might possibly be complaints from parents who do not know when they are well off." Grinning, Stinker Larsen looked from one to the other of us, and finally selected one of the bigger boys, to whom he handed his own suitcase, politely requesting him to carry it.

"Good old Stinker." Nikolai nudged me. "That will

fix the Lighthouse; he would have wanted us to march like an infantry battalion. Stinker is a conservative, but he is all right."

Nikolai had a habit of adding a person's politics immediately following their names, like addresses or telephone numbers.

On our way to the Youth Hostel, we saw several youngsters our own age in the uniform of the Hitler Youth. Each time we passed one, Nikolai would sneer, "To hell with Hitler." But he said it in Danish and not very loud.

The Youth Hostel was a modern, L-shaped building with a courtyard. We were quartered in two dormitories on the second floor. Along the walls double-decker bunks were arranged in an orderly fashion. Nikolai and I were lucky enough to get corner ones; I took the upper and he the lower. It was strange the way we had paired off; after all, that morning, we had never heard of each other, and now we were best friends.

I threw my suitcase up onto my bunk and climbed up after it. Now I would have a chance to see what was in the package—but I would have to be careful. I pushed the suitcase into the corner, and then looked around. It was rather fun having an upper bunk and looking down on the boys passing below. Some of them were already busy with their luggage. No one would notice if I looked into mine.

I had turned my back to the room and was just about to open my suitcase, when right behind me I heard someone clear his throat. I knew immediately that it was not a boy but a grownup. At the end of my bed, staring at me, was the Lighthouse. Because of the secret which my suitcase contained, I blushed guiltily, as if I had been caught committing a crime.

"I just wanted to tell you, Erik Hansen . . . and you . . ." The Lighthouse's shoulders were flush with my bunk and he had to bend down to look at the occupant of the lower accommodation. "I have forgotten your name—what is it?"

"Nikolai Karl Leon Linde. The Nikolai comes from my grandfather, I inherited it a week after I was born, the rest of the names—"

"Shut up!" Nikolai's voice had been friendly to excess; the Lighthouse's was not friendly at all. "I want you two to behave yourselves. This is the home of the German youth. While you are here, I will hear no disparaging remarks from you about our hosts! Is that understood?"

"Yes," I whispered, and waited for Nikolai to shout "*jawohl*" or "*Heil* Hitler." But for once he showed some good sense, and the Lighthouse left us feeling that we had been properly put in our place.

He had no sooner left the room than Nikolai was out on the floor, with outstretched hand, saying, "*Jawohl, Überführer!*"

I told him to shut up, which earned me a "*Jawohl, Unterführer.*"

When I finally untied the package in my suitcase, I almost didn't dare to look inside. The wrapping was of ordinary brown paper, though of a very heavy kind. I do not know what I had expected to find—jewels, gold, or the plans for the fortification of Copenhagen harbor—but I was more than a little disappointed when I unfolded the paper and exposed two stacks of Danish passports.

36

5   The Locked Store

"How many were there?" Nikolai asked, after I had finished telling him about the package and how it had come into my hands.

"Fifty," I answered. "They are all without photographs and stamps, as if they had just come from the printer's."

"Oh, those stamps of a rural police office would be easy enough to counterfeit. Do you know how valuable such a passport would be to someone who had to flee from Germany?" Nikolai made a low whistle. "You have got a fortune in your suitcase."

"You know the blind men who sell pencils in the railroad stations? They have them on a tray in front of them. Maybe I could sell passports that way!" I laughed; but then, because it was not really a laughing matter at all, I asked, "Do you think *he* was going to sell them?"

"No." Nikolai shook his head. "He didn't look like that kind of fellow."

"What did he look like? Do you remember?" I pleaded. We were sitting in a corner of the dining room in the Youth Hostel; all the others had long since finished their breakfasts and we were alone.

"He was slight of build . . . and not tall. I think his hair was fair . . . and a bit thin, as though he were growing bald. I remember his raincoat; the collar was all frayed and one button was missing."

"I know," I interrupted. "It's that damned raincoat that one remembers and not what was inside it. Why is that?"

"Because he was so ordinary, maybe." Nikolai paused. "I mean, you always look for something to remember someone by, and then there wasn't anything, so we both grabbed onto the raincoat."

"But he wasn't ordinary, he just looked it." This thought gave me great pleasure—after all, I looked pretty ordinary myself—and I wanted to enlarge upon it. "Take the Lighthouse," I began.

"You take him." Nikolai was scowling.

"He is pretty ordinary, but he doesn't look it."

"He does to me." Nikolai was not being very cooperative. "I think *he* was a Comrade," he said slowly.

"A Comrade?" I asked. "What do you mean?"

"I mean he was a Communist like my father. You could see that he was working class." Nikolai nodded to emphasize the truth of what he was saying.

"How do you know?" I said, rebelling. "Just because

38

he wore a shabby coat! Why do you always have to talk about everybody's politics, as if that mattered!"

Nikolai stared at me as though he had never seen me before; and then he repeated my words in solemn wonder. "As if that mattered . . ."

"Yes," I argued, defending my point of view. "What really matters is whether you are a decent person or not."

"Like a decent fascist?" he asked sarcastically.

"Well, no!" I gave up my point of view reluctantly. As so often with Nikolai, at one and the same time, I felt that I was defeated and that I was right. Instinctively, I knew what I meant by "decent," but I also knew that I would not be able to explain it without sounding like a Sunday-school teacher.

"Boys!" Stinker Larsen stuck his head inside the door. "Come along, you are about to be taken on an edifying tour of the city."

As we filed past him, the teacher put his hand on Nikolai's shoulder. "There is an old saying that one should howl with the wolves whose company one is in." He shook his head. "I don't believe that; I don't think that you should keep company with wolves at all. But if you are forced to, then at least you should keep your mouth shut and not go around bleating like sheep."

I nodded to let him know that I understood, which I was not completely certain that I had; but Nikolai had to air his opinions. "Wolves belong in the zoo, sir," he said.

"And so do monkeys." Stinker Larsen grinned good-naturedly. "Come along, and we shall see if we can't find a cage for you."

"Is Germany a zoo, sir?" Nikolai persisted.

The teacher looked at my friend as though he were making up his mind what kind of monkey he might be. His cheerful, round face, which seemed made for smiling, was suddenly serious. "Yes," he said, "I think it is. But remember one thing, boys, you are not on the *outside* looking in, you are *inside* the cage yourselves. There are no bars to protect you from the tiger prowling in the night." Stinker Larsen's hand still rested on Nikolai's shoulder. "We will do what we can to help you, if you get into trouble; but there is no reason to get a beating for nothing, so keep your opinions to yourselves. I, least of anyone, would like to hear you shouting '*Heil* Hitler' from the rooftops. I am merely suggesting that you be sensible." Giving Nikolai a gentle shove, he turned and walked away.

"He is all right, but he is frightened." Nikolai grimaced. "That is the trouble with liberals, they are a frightened lot."

For the first time I was really angry with Nikolai. "Stinker Larsen is exactly what I meant when I said 'a decent man,' " I sputtered, and turning my back on him, I followed the teacher down into the courtyard where the other boys were assembled.

"Lübeck was the most important of the towns in the Hanseatic League, even more important than Hamburg." We were all flocked around the Lighthouse, on the square in front of the old Town Hall. Nikolai was standing as close to me as he could, but I ignored him, and acted as though

I were intensely interested in the facts. Mr. Nielsen was flinging at us so enthusiastically.

"The Hanseatic League reached the height of its power in the thirteenth and fourteenth centuries. Parts of the Town Hall date back to the thirteenth century. The Marienkirche—" the Lighthouse pointed in the direction of that beautiful church—"was built in the latter half of the thirteenth century and the early years of the fourteenth. For twenty-five years, in the beginning of the thirteenth century, Lübeck was—" Now the Lighthouse's arm made a sweeping movement that took in all the medieval houses and churches of the city, while he paused rhetorically; then, breathing deeply, he began his sentence again, "Lübeck was Danish!"

I don't know whether he was expecting applause; but if so, he must have been disappointed.

"You would think it had belonged to him personally," Nikolai whispered.

I shrugged my shoulders, indicating that I had heard what he said but did not think it worthy of comment.

"I am sorry," he whispered next. "I know I am a bit of an ass."

I turned and smiled, for in truth I was already sorry that we had disagreed, but I was relieved that it was he and not I who offered an apology.

Nikolai held out his hand and I grasped it. "We are the Popular Front," he said and laughed.

Nikolai was looking up at me, as if he wanted to gauge my reaction to what he was going to say before he said it. "My parents were very poor."

We were walking through the narrow streets of Lübeck. It was late in the afternoon, but there was still a while before we had to return to the Youth Hostel for dinner, which was at six o'clock.

"They often went hungry when they were children—at least, that's what they say. My grandfather died while my father was still a boy and my grandmother was a—" Nikolai hesitated before he said "laundrywoman," then he corrected himself and said "washerwoman."

I nodded because I felt sure that anything I might say would be wrong. I was both pleased and embarrassed at being deemed worthy of his confidence.

"My father was a Social Democrat for many years, and so was my mother; but not long after they got married, he joined the party." Nikolai always referred to the *party,* as if there were no political movement but the Communist. "That is why I am called Karl Leon."

"Oh," I said, trying to give the impression that this made sense to me, but Nikolai saw the confusion on my face.

"The Karl was after Karl Marx and the Leon after Trotsky. Have you read *Das Kapital?*"

For a fleeting moment, I thought of answering in the affirmative, but since I had only heard of Karl Marx and Leon Trotsky was a totally unknown quantity to me, I decided not to.

"I haven't either." Nikolai laughed. "But if you had said you had, I would have said I had, too. Do you ever lie about what you have read?" Nikolai had a habit of asking embarrassing questions.

"Sometimes," I said. "But not to my parents because they wouldn't care."

"Then who do you lie to?" We had come to a corner and had stopped before crossing the street.

"To myself," I answered in a low voice, when we had reached the other side. "I told myself that I had read *War and Peace*; but I hadn't really, I had skipped a lot of pages." It wasn't that I didn't know what kind of boy I wanted to be, but that I found it difficult to live up to my ideal. With my birthday money, I had bought a copy of *The Brothers Karamazov* and had it lying on my desk. But I hadn't read it; instead I had been reading Captain Marryat's *Midshipman Easy*. I blushed, for it was such a silly secret to reveal.

Nikolai, perhaps to rescue me from my embarrassment, declared that he lied like that all the time—but mostly to his parents.

Walking aimlessly, we now found ourselves in a very poor part of the town. The street was so narrow that it would better be described as an alley. The houses were tall and left but a narrow shaft for the sun to shine down through. There was an unpleasant, musty air, as if no wind ever disturbed the damp atmosphere.

A shop window caught the attention of both of us at the same time. Across it was pasted a paper banner that declared in bold letters: NO GERMAN BUYS IN JEWISH SHOPS. On the walls of the house I now noticed that other messages had been written with chalk or paint; I couldn't tell which. Clumsily printed, with even simple words misspelled, they looked like the ones on lavatory walls.

43

It was a very small store, the kind you can find in the old parts of Copenhagen, with the owner living in the back room.

"Let's go in and buy something!" Nikolai had his hand on the handle of the door, but it was locked.

A woman's face appeared at the window of a house across the street. 'She may think that we have come to do harm,' I thought, 'that we might write something on the door or the wall.' And I shivered. "Come," I said aloud to Nikolai. "Let's go back." I looked up and down the almost dark alley; it was empty.

"Swine!" Nikolai mumbled. "Fascist . . . Nazi . . . Swine!" And with his fingers, he tried to pull the streamer off the window; but it had been there a long time and was very securely glued. From his trouser pocket, Nikolai drew a small penknife and started to scrape the paper off.

"Don't," said a voice behind us. "Please don't." A boy about our own age, with a thin, white face and brown hair as long as I would have liked to wear mine, if my mother would have let me, was standing in the middle of the lane.

Suddenly his face flushed, as if he felt ashamed. "You see," he explained, "they will come back and see that their sign has been torn off the window, and then they will throw a stone through it. Or . . ." The boy looked down at the cobblestones. "Or they will break down the door. The man who lives in there is very old."

Nikolai closed his penknife and put it back into his pocket. "But one must do something," he exclaimed, and then he muttered once more, "They are swine!"

The boy shrugged his shoulders, as if to say, so what. For one mad moment, I wanted to give him money, as if that could help; but then I was brought up in a home where any problem could be solved in that manner.

The boy gave a smile to each of us, and we smiled back, as if we were exchanging precious gifts; then he turned and went back into the house he had come from and closed the door behind him.

Again Nikolai in his dumb anger called upon that innocent beast with the corkscrew tail whom we like to abuse. I pointed to an inscription on the wall beside the shop door; there dabbed in red letters was that very animal's name.

"Maybe the passports are for someone like him," I said and nodded towards the house in which the boy lived. And suddenly I knew that I would have to try and deliver them to the address that the man in the gray raincoat had given me, for if I didn't, I would die of shame.

6   The Knife

On our way back to the Youth Hostel, I tried to explain to Nikolai that nothing must stand in the way of our delivering the passports. He readily agreed with me, but when I pointed out to him that this would mean that he would have to guard his tongue, he chose at first to be offended.

"Do I have to shout *Heil* Hitler?" he grumbled, which was absurd and he knew it. "Maybe you would like me to goosestep," he continued angrily, as he lifted his legs high into the air, in that particularly ridiculous form of marching which makes soldiers look as if they were puppets.

"Stop it!" I exclaimed. "That is exactly what I don't want you to do. Don't draw attention to yourself. The Lighthouse is down on us as it is . . . Look!" Just then I happened to notice that a group of boys dressed in the uniform of the Hitler Youth were watching us.

46

"You are right," Nikolai admitted, crestfallen. "I just can't help it." He grinned at me. "My father says that I am the kind of person who insists upon discussing shoes with a man who has a wooden leg."

"Well, don't discuss anything with anybody until that package is safely delivered."

"My father claims that it is because he gave me the name Leon that I am the way I am. He says that was his big mistake—he should have called me Joseph instead."

"Why?" I asked, because I still was very confused about all of Nikolai's names.

"Well, Karl—as I have already told you—comes from Karl Marx, which is fine and traditional, just as the bourgeoisie call their sons Christian after the king, which doesn't make them into princes."

I winced, for my middle name was Christian, but Nikolai did not seem to notice.

"Now Leon is another matter. I think I told you that before, too—but I was baptized Leon after Trotsky." Nikolai shook his head. "It was a very sad mistake on my father's part, but how was he to know?"

"To know what?" I asked.

"You mean—" Nikolai stood still and stopped talking to study the expression on my face—"that you don't know who Leon Trotsky is?"

"No, is that frightfully stupid of me? I hardly ever read the newspapers."

"This is wonderful . . . I must tell my father about it. But he probably won't believe me." Nikolai gazed at me in wonder as though he didn't believe it himself.

"But, as I have already told you, my parents don't take

any interest in politics. I mean, we never talk about it."

To my surprise, Nikolai's face grew grave. "You don't know how lucky you are," he said. "My father—and my mother, too—talk nothing but politics. It is all they live for. Do you know who Lenin was?"

"Yes, he started the Russian revolution," I said with relief, and tried to remember what else I might know about Lenin. All I could recall was a photograph in which he had been bald, but I had the good sense not to disclose this obvious but important historical fact out loud.

"Well, my sister is called Ninel." Nikolai sighed.

"That's a nice name," I said honestly.

"It is Lenin spelled backwards." Nikolai stamped his foot. "My sister is two years older than I am. My father wanted a son very badly so he could name him Lenin, instead he got a daughter . . . hocus pocus! Ninel is a female Lenin."

Nikolai looked so funny that I could not help laughing. "If you had come first, you would have been Lenin and your sister would have been Karla Leona."

"No, she wouldn't have been; she would have been Rosa like my younger sister. She was named after Rosa Luxemburg."

"And who is she?"

"*Was* . . . She is dead."

As we neared the Youth Hostel we began to walk even more slowly. "You are lucky, you know," Nikolai said, "to have parents who don't care. Whenever I think of my sister's name, I can't help laughing." I glanced at Nikolai; he was grinning from ear to ear. "When Lenin

48

died, they stuffed him and put him in a glass cage just as our zoology teacher did with an owl he had found. Then they built a great mausoleum for him, and there he lies like Snow White in a glass coffin. My father went all the way to Moscow, as if he were one of the Seven Dwarfs. And when he came back, he said it was an inspiring sight and brought me a stack of postcards. That was a year ago, and that is when I made up my mind to become an anarchist . . . You know, I wonder about it, do you think that all grownups are crazy?"

"I don't know . . . Some of them are, I guess." I touched Nikolai's shoulder. "But it's not only grownups who are crazy. Look what's coming."

Just about to enter the gate of the Youth Hostel from the opposite direction were a group of Hitler Youth. Kurt, a boy from my class, had his arm around one of them.

"It's the uniform," Nikolai commented. "That is the bait that will catch a lot of codfish."

I was eager to get back to our dormitory to make sure that no one had tampered with my suitcase. "Leave them alone, Nikolai; especially Kurt, for I trust him least of all."

My suitcase had not been touched. Since there was still a quarter of an hour until dinner, I took off my shoes and lay down in my bunk. It was nice to lie there staring up at the ceiling; in one corner there was a cobweb. I strained my eyes to find the spider, but the web was old.

I wished that I had said something to the boy we had met, but even now I couldn't find anything to say beyond that I was sorry, and that wasn't only because I had to say it in German.

What would it be like to live in a house decorated with insults, and then on top of it, not dare to take them off for fear of something worse happening? He had been a Jew; what did that mean to me? Wasn't it like being an Egyptian? That was romantic. The Old Testament was all about Jews—I was not so ignorant that I did not know that. Twice a week we had religion in school; but since we were never examined in it, like the rest of the boys I used that hour for studying math or some other important subject. We would keep our books beneath our desks, but our teacher usually knew what we were up to.

"Put your book on top of your desk, or you will ruin your eyes," he would say in the kindliest of tones. And we, for a little while, would be shamed into putting our books away and listening to him. He was the minister at the largest jail in Denmark; and in my imagination, I would see him in the cell of a condemned murderer who was to be hanged the following morning—and that in spite of the fact that the death penalty had been abolished in Denmark for more than half a century.

Suddenly I remembered that there was a Jew in my class. His name was Solomonsen. His father was a schoolteacher, and his mother a nurse. I had visited them once at Christmastime and they had had a Christmas tree that was a good foot taller than ours. The boy's name was Hans, that was Danish, so maybe he wasn't Jewish after all, and it was just something someone had said.

50

Leaning over the side of my bunk, I asked Nikolai, "Do you know any Jews?"

"Leon Trotsky," he replied brightly. "And then there's a girl who plays with my sister, her name is Eva Cohen. People say that the Jews are Communists, but my father says that's just propaganda—they're mostly Social Democrats."

I was feeling sleepy. My eyes closed, but a moment later, Kurt and some of his friends stormed into the room, making enough noise to wake, if not the dead, then at least the soundest of sleepers.

I sat up and glanced at my watch: in five minutes we would be called for dinner. I jumped down from my bunk and put on my shoes; my mind was on what we were going to be given to eat. The food in the Youth Hostel left much to be desired, but then I was used to good food. My father was a gourmet, or at least he thought he was.

Kurt was standing by his bunk, with a group of admirers around him. I don't know why I walked over to join them, for I didn't like Kurt, and we had little, if anything, in common. He was an enthusiastic gymnast, a prejudice that I might have forgiven him—after all, everyone should be allowed a vice or two—but what was unforgivable was that after gymnastics, when the obligatory shower was just about over, he would drench his towel in water and use it as a weapon upon some innocent and unsuspecting boy's bare behind. I had been his victim many times, and it was not a form of humor I shared. Kurt was a bit of a bully, but not a particularly nasty one; he was not the kind who waited outside the school

51

in order to tyrannize some poor weakling on his way home. He was in truth just an ordinary boy; there were many other knights of the wet towel in my class. They would fight each other like puppies. My trouble was that I believed that I belonged to the human rather than the canine species.

Kurt was showing something to the other boys; perhaps that had been the reason for my approaching him. I was curious, nosy.

"Isn't it a beauty?" one of the boys asked me and held out a sleek-looking dagger. Its shaft was black and in the middle of the handle was an enamel shield with a swastika in it. The blade was eight inches long, and into its shiny surface had been engraved three words: BLUT UND EHRE . . . Blood and Honor.

I took it in my hand and looked at it. I had a sheath knife which my father had brought me from Norway; it was a pretty little knife with a bone handle and a blade not half the size of this one. I never used it for anything except to clean my fingernails; but I decided right then and there that I would give it away when I got home.

"It is the Führer's handwriting." The boy out of whose hand I had taken the knife spoke with reverence.

I looked at Kurt and he at me. I wanted to say that I had not known Hitler could write; but I decided, considering the warning I had given poor Nikolai, that it would hardly be diplomatic. Instead I remarked as casually as I could, "I don't see what the two have to do with each other."

"You wouldn't," Kurt sniffed arrogantly. "Those who associate with Jews seldom know what honor means."

"What the hell are you talking about?" I shouted in surprise. Had Kurt been following us and seen us talking to the Jewish boy? I was sure the street had been empty.

"Didn't you know that your constant companion is a Jew?" Kurt sneered as he held up his palm for me to return the knife.

"If Nikolai is a Jew then so am I!" I said angrily, handing it back to him.

As I walked down the stairs to the dining hall, I suddenly remembered that I did know of one man who for certain was a Jew, for our German teacher, himself, had said so: Heinrich Heine. He had been a Jew and I liked his poetry. I was going to be a poet myself one day. And of this I was convinced, Kurt and his friends were the enemies of poets.

7   The Bookstore

There was no doubt about it—the boys were breaking up into three distinct groups. One of them, led by Kurt, was definitely what Nikolai called "fascists." It was not numerous, but it was larger than the third group whom Nikolai named the "anti-fascists." Most of the boys did not belong to either bunch, and had I not met Nikolai Karl Leon Linde and the man in the gray raincoat, I, too, would have belonged to this group in the middle. Nikolai called them Mensheviks, another of those strange words that meant nothing to me but were part and parcel of Nikolai's vocabulary; to my surprise he had more contempt for them than he did for the fascists. It annoyed me and I asked him why he should hate those who in many ways were the most innocent of all of us.

"That you dislike Kurt, I can understand. I wouldn't care for him under any circumstances; but you seem to resent even more those who do no one any harm and have no interest in politics."

"Politics!" Nikolai sputtered. "Nazism is not politics, it is mass criminality! Not to fight it makes you guilty of supporting it."

"That's something your father said," I replied with contempt; Nikolai had sounded so much like a parrot.

"So what!" Nikolai was getting angry as well. "I know he is only a stoker, but that doesn't mean that he isn't right sometimes."

Until then I had not realized that Nikolai was as ashamed of his father as I was of mine. It had never before occurred to me that the calamity of having parents who did not measure up to one's standard was not experienced by me alone, but was probably a universal misfortune.

Somewhat mollified, I said, "Oh, your father could be right. Parents are sometimes . . . I just wish you wouldn't be so hard on the others."

Nikolai shrugged his shoulders as if to say, 'I will think about that.'

This was our third and final day in Lübeck. The next day we would take the train to Hamburg, for which I was not sorry. I imagined myself walking into the Golden Lamb and saying that I was a friend of Christian Wahnschaffe. It was romantic, like something in Dumas's *The Three Musketeers*. I thought of myself as d'Artagnan. Yet I was eager for it to be over with. I wanted to be rid of those passports.

It was early afternoon and I was lying on my bunk, just a few minutes after my argument with Nikolai. 'He is right,' I admitted to myself, 'not to fight fascism is to support it. But there are times when I feel that Nikolai likes violence too, that somehow his pleasure in the fight makes him a little akin to Kurt.' But I had no sooner thought this than I felt ashamed of myself, as if I were a traitor to a cause that I knew to be right. The trouble was that to play cops and robbers was amusing, so long as you were playing; but the boy with the long dark hair, who lived in the alley, and the man in the gray raincoat were not taking part in a game.

"Come on, we're free for the rest of the afternoon," Nikolai called. Two of his friends from the "anti-fascist brigade" had joined him—one of them was from my school. "We don't have to be back before six."

"I don't feel like going out. I think I'll stay here and read."

Nikolai bit his lip. I knew he wanted me along, but I picked up my book and said casually, "Have a good time."

I knew what they were up to. In the morning we had had an hour to ourselves, as well. Nikolai had led us to one shop after another, and when the owner—or whoever it was that waited on us—said, "*Heil* Hitler!" we had replied in a chorus, "*Grüss Gott!*" Usually the "*Heil* Hitler*" was repeated, and we responded as before with our "*Grüss Gott.*" At this point young shop assistants would turn their backs on us, and there the matter ended. But in one toy shop, Nikolai had bought a clay figure of Hitler from an elderly woman for 20 pfennigs. She had slipped it carefully into a paper bag. As soon as his purchase was in his hands, Nikolai opened the bag as if it contained candy, and he were in doubt as to which piece he preferred. Finally, he pulled out the Führer by the legs, and placing the little pottery head in his mouth, he allowed his teeth to play the guillotine; then he spit the severed head out on the floor and returned the paper bag with the headless torso to the confused old woman. Luckily for us, she was the only witness to this scene. The six or seven boys who were with us had been most impressed; and now I thought cynically, 'Maybe that was the whole purpose of the comedy.' I was still angry about it, for if there had been a group of Hitler *Jugend* in the store, we certainly would have been beaten up, and for what? For the pleasure of shocking an old lady who probably had not understood why we were behaving that way in the first place. 'Naughty Danish boys, not like our German ones, who know how to behave,' is most likely what she thought. At least until the passports were delivered, I did not intend to partake in any more of Nikolai's nonsense.

So you see, I had not decided to stay at the Youth Hostel because my book was so exciting that I couldn't put it down. It was eminently put-downable; Nikolai and his friends had not been gone fifteen minutes before I was lying on my back staring at the ceiling. This was of even less interest than the printed page, and since there were several hours before dinner, I made up my mind to explore the city by myself.

It is good to be with friends, but from the point of view of observing a strange place, it is better to be alone. For the first time I became aware that almost every young person was wearing some kind of uniform; of the men, only those as old as my father wore ordinary clothes. The flags and buntings in national colors that decorated the buildings I am sure I have mentioned before, but I had not paid any attention to the streamers with slogans on them. They were filled with catchwords that were meant, I presumed, to bolster national pride, but I wondered how many people actually took the time to read them.

I was passing a book store; on display were copies of *Mein Kampf*. In the center of them was a picture of the author in a gold frame. I stared at him, and from his photograph Hitler stared back at me. His was a strangely lifeless face. 'How is it possible?' I asked myself unbelievingly. 'How?'

"That is *unser Führer!*" A short, bald man was standing beside me. He smiled up at me and then at the picture in the window.

'It is the word *unser,* "our," that is even more important than *Führer,*' I thought. 'The Germans love a leader, I had heard even my father say that. Maybe Hitler is theirs in a way the Kaiser never was.'

"Where are you from?" the man asked politely.

"Denmark," I answered, while involuntarily, I straightened myself like a soldier on parade.

"A beautiful country." He almost bowed and I agreed that Denmark, indeed, was *schön.*

"*Bitte.*" The man lifted his green, curiously fuzzy hat, and this time he did bow before he replaced it on his head (which was only sparsely covered by hair) and walked away.

I cast one more glance at *unser Führer,* half expecting that now he would smile contentedly; but he was still stupidly staring straight ahead.

It is difficult to explain what happened to me next without pleading my own sort of stupidity.

I came across a secondhand bookstore. It had the right kind of musty atmosphere that makes you think of eternity without either pain or fear. Through the window I could just make out a few human figures between the high rows of bookcases. I went inside and started to examine the volumes on the shelves. Some had lovely leather bindings. But a quick glance at the pages made me realize how little German, in truth, I knew. I could no more than hazard a guess as to what most of the books were about; and some of them might just as well have been written in Greek.

"Are you looking for something in particular?"

The voice, coming from behind, made me jump; the gaze of the man, who I was convinced was the owner of the shop as well as its only salesman, made me feel as though I had been detected in the act of trying to steal something.

"*Bitte,* have you got the poems of Heinrich Heine?" I said, merely because I did not know what else to ask for; in our German class in school we had just been reading his poetry.

"Get out!" the man screamed at me, while pointing to the door.

"*Entschuldigung* . . . Excuse me . . ." I kept repeating as I backed towards the entrance.

The shopkeeper followed me, while spouting German at me as fast as a river in flood. I understood very little but the word *Jude* was repeated many times.

When I finally found myself outside on the sidewalk, I

was so stunned that I stood perfectly still. An elderly customer with gold-rimmed glasses, whom I had noticed because he had reminded me of one of my schoolteachers, was hurrying out of the shop. Obviously, he had come to talk with me, because he smiled with relief when he saw me.

"Please follow me," he said in a voice not much above a whisper. Once we had turned the corner and could no longer be seen from the bookstore, he stopped and looked at me intently. "Did you really not know that Heinrich Heine was a Jewish, not a German, poet?"

Somehow I managed to meet his glance, so you see it is not true that one cannot look another in the face and lie. "We are taught that he is German in our school . . . in Denmark," I said, for how could I possibly have explained to him or anyone else—even myself!—that I had forgotten it? That I had said Heine's name because his was the first that came into my mind? Since the old man continued to stare at me, I added defensively, "I like his poetry very much."

"*Jawohl . . . Jawohl . . .*" The old man bobbed his head up and down just like the Chinese porcelain doll that stood on the mantelpiece in my aunt's house; then he took off his glasses and wiped them carefully. To my great surprise I saw a tear running down his cheek; it ran crookedly, following a wrinkle.

"*Ach so . . .*" he said as he put the glasses back on. "If a man is very cold on the North Pole, he cannot believe that somewhere else palm trees are growing and flowers are blooming. It is so with us here in Germany . . .

60

Yet—," he shook his finger at me—"all that is present will one day be past; nothing lasts forever."

I did not know what to say. The single tear that I had seen on his face had made me want to say something comforting; but I could think of nothing, and I smiled rather foolishly.

"Come with me," the old man commanded rather than suggested. Silently we walked side by side through the narrow streets of Lübeck, until we came to one of those old half-timbered houses whose second floor juts out over the first. Here he stopped and, as he took out a key, bade me wait for his return. Before he closed the door behind him, I caught a glimpse of a narrow corridor and a carved staircase.

I kept looking at my watch, so I know that I did not stand there more than fifteen minutes, but it felt like an hour. It seemed to me that some of the people who passed on the street were looking at me suspiciously, as if each of them were thinking, 'I must remember that young fellow's face because he is up to something that he shouldn't be.' I felt as conspicuous as if I were eight feet tall.

The door of the house was very old; I believe it was made of oak. It had six panels, each with a different flower carved in it. I remember thinking, 'It must have taken a terribly long time to decorate that door. Surely today no one would bother to do it.' I had just decided that the old man had forgotten me when the door finally opened.

The old man waited until the street was empty, then

61

he held out a very small package wrapped in brown paper, which I could see had been used before because there were fold marks in the wrong places.

"Here," he said, "you take this back to Dänemark. It was my grandfather's."

Had he given me a chance, I might have protested. After all, I did not know what was in the package; besides, I could not help feeling that I had been given packages enough already. But he quickly patted my cheek and said that I was a good boy. The way he did it made me certain that he was or had been a schoolteacher. Then, as if he were fleeing from the "good boy," he turned, walked into his house, and closed the door behind him.

I slipped the package into my pocket and retraced my steps. It was time to return to the Youth Hostel.

As I approached the gate, I suddenly smiled, remembering that I had refused to go with Nikolai because I hadn't wanted to partake in his sport, and then I had unwittingly played just such a trick in the secondhand bookstore as would have delighted my friend. I decided that I had better not tell him of my adventure, for if I did, he would drag me through all the bookstores in Hamburg when we arrived there.

The others had not yet returned. As soon as I was up in my bunk, I opened my package. I was right, the paper had been used before; on the reverse side there was a name and an address. I wondered whether it was the old man's; it might have been, but I would never know for certain. The string, too, was not on its first journey, for it was two pieces tied together.

What I had unwrapped was a little book. On its title page was printed: *Deutschland: Ein Wintermärchen*; beneath that was the author's name, and at the very bottom, the year of publication: 1844.

To my surprise, when I turned back to the flyleaf I saw that there was something written in ink. It was faded and brown: a name and then some words that I could not quite make out and then another name. It was a dedication, and the second name was easy to decipher, for it was the same name that appeared on the title page—Heinrich Heine.

I sat for a long time with the book in my hands. 'Such a signature is like a handshake from the grave,' I thought. Even though it could never have been dedicated to me, I somehow felt as if it had been. I put it away in my suitcase on top of the passports, and whispered aloud rather foolishly, "It was given to me . . . to me!"

8   The Parade

Nikolai looked at me aggressively. "Have you heard?" he asked.

"Heard what?" I replied. Having two ears and normal hearing, I had heard a good deal above the din of the dining hall, which we were in the process of departing from.

"We are to have an evening of friendship with the fascists!" Nikolai reeked disgust. "It is all the Lighthouse's idea."

"*Gemütlich*," I said and grinned. *Gemütlich* is one of those words that cannot be translated; it is specifically German. It is constructed from sing-alongs, folk dancing, and friendliness, all spelled in toto with capital letters. It is to be found at Boy Scout Jamborees and among grownups in beer halls late at night, when they link arms and sing, "For he's a jolly good fellow ..." It is the lowing of the herd when it is content. Naturally, I hated it and Nikolai at least hated being *gemütlich* with people whose politics he did not approve of.

"I don't know whether I am going." Nikolai folded his arms across his chest. If he had had a lock of hair falling down over his forehead, he would have looked like Napoleon.

"Don't be silly," I said. "It will be interesting." This wasn't really the way I felt at all, for I hated sing-alongs as much as I did gymnastics, but I did not want Nikolai to make any trouble by refusing to go.

"You know what he has called it: the evening of brotherhood!" Nikolai spat out the last word.

"Well, what's wrong with that? Most brothers that I know of are always fighting." Being an only child who had wished very much for a brother, I had always noticed anything that could make my singleness more bearable.

"Have you seen Pind?" Nikolai asked.

Pind means "twig" in Danish; and this particular boy, who was in my class, had been nicknamed Pind because he was as thin as one. He was to be pitied. Not only had he been born with a harelip, but his head was huge and looked like the dwarf's in a book of fairytales. He was not stupid, but he was not a clever boy either; and unfortunately, of all the Danish boys, he seemed the most infected by the atmosphere around us. He had bought not only a knife but all sorts of Nazi regalia. He appeared to delight in the superiority of the Nordic, or as he called them, "the Germanic races." It was ridiculous to hear him, with his lisp, exclaiming the virtues of the Aryan over the *Untermenschen;* and he embarrassed Kurt so much that he would not allow him to be one of his followers.

"He is pathetic," I said, and I meant it.

"He is disgusting," said Nikolai, and he meant it too. "Had he been a puppy or a kitten, he would have been drowned at birth."

"Yes." I nodded. "I suspect that he knows that too; he's been told so often enough. I can forgive him, but I cannot forgive Kurt and his gang. Besides, the Twig makes the whole thing absurd. Every time I see him with his dagger, his Nazi tie clip, and all the rest of his nonsense, I feel like laughing."

"If you were the Jewish boy we met in the alley, you wouldn't think that Twig was so funny," Nikolai replied angrily.

"I don't particularly want to defend Twig; he's a bloody fool. That's not my point," I said, warming up to my argument. "What I can't see is why it should be more disgusting for a poor gnome with a harelip and water on the brain to be a Nazi than it is for a strong, healthy lout like Kurt. I find that twenty-six and a half times more disgusting! And if you ask me, you are being prejudiced. The Twig may be a worm, but at least he looks like one, which should be counted in his favor." Somehow the latter part of my argument had come unstuck; even I felt that there was something wrong with it, but happily Nikolai did not seem to notice.

"Maybe they will make us sing the *Horst Wessel*," Nikolai grumbled.

"Even if they used Chinese torture, they couldn't make

66

me sing it," I declared with a laugh because I was so glad that we had gotten off the subject of Twig.

"I wouldn't be too sure of that, they might try it," Nikolai said darkly.

"Since I don't know the words and don't know the melody and can't sing, I don't see how." I stretched myself as we stepped outside into the courtyard of the Youth Hostel.

"They have their ways . . . They will roast the soles of your feet over an open fire . . ." Nikolai shook his head sadly. "And when you scream like a pig, you have sung the *Horst Wessel*. Did you know that that Nazi hero was a pimp?"

"No, because this is the first time I have heard of him. And what's more I don't care if he was the illegitimate son of Hitler and the Kaiser."

"Du bist ein Dummkopf!" Nikolai's German accent was worse than mine.

"Auch du bist ein . . . ein . . ." Out of the mist of my ignorance two words finally arrived at the same time: *"Ein Idiot Esel!"*

"You are both donkeys." Stinker Larsen was standing right behind us. He put one hand on Nikolai's shoulder and the other on mine. "But I prefer that animal to monkeys."

"Sir, do we have to go to that party this evening?" Nikolai asked.

The teacher frowned. "It wasn't my idea," he said, "but it would be best you came; then you could *not* sing, *not* talk, and *not* be friendly to the Hitler *Jugend* . . . I won't tell you not to come. You are free to stay in the dormitory, but if only those who agree with our little brown-shirted friends or have no opinions in such matters attend, it could easily be misunderstood."

"Will you be there?" I asked.

"I shall." Stinker Larsen grinned. "But it's just possible that the smell of so many little boys might make me sick; if that should happen, I will leave and you might leave with me . . . You might tell that to anyone whom you consider your friends." Giving our backs a final, friendly pat, the teacher walked on.

"I like him." Nikolai breathed the words rather than spoke them. "If the Lighthouse goes too far, and they all start *Heil*ing, we will all leave when Stinker gives the cue. We had better go and tell the others . . . It would look pretty bad if only the three of us walked out."

Friendliness and brotherhood had been planned to last from eight o'clock until ten; then a parade of the Hitler *Jugend* of Lübeck was to take place that would deprive us of our brothers and friends, as they were scheduled to take part in it.

Both hosts and guests behaved themselves. We sang folk songs until nine-thirty, when we drank cocoa and ate buns supplied by the Third Reich. Although we had been told to take only one each of both, Nikolai drank two cups of cocoa and ate three buns; but when I said something to him about it, he defended his greed by declaring that by taking three buns he had assured that two Nazis would go hungry.

Throughout the get-together, the Lighthouse was

seated between the two Hitler *Jugend* leaders with whom he conversed with great gusto.

I asked one of our uniformed hosts, a short dark-haired boy with glasses, what they called their leaders.

"Unsere Gebietsführer," he answered and almost came to attention.

Now *Gebiets,* which in German means "of the district," sounds very much like the Danish word for false teeth, *Gebiss;* this amused me and I looked around for Nikolai to tell him about it for future reference. But I couldn't see him anywhere; and suddenly I realized that the Hitler Youth was talking to me; he wanted to know what we called our leaders.

I took out my Danish–German pocket dictionary and looked up the words for Lighthouse. *"Der Leuchtturm,"* I said and pointed at the beanstalk. The German boy grinned as if I had told a dirty joke; but when I managed to find the word for Stinker and explained that our other teacher was called, *"Der Gestank Larsen,"* he moved away with a frightened expression on his face.

At precisely five minutes to ten, all the young Germans exclaimed that they had had a grand time, and each one shook the hand of the Danish boy nearest him. I seemed to have got myself in a corner sadly lacking in Danes, so I had to shake hands with six Hitler *Jugenden,* there being no one else around to perform the chore. Perhaps this handshaking ceremony was obligatory, and their *Gebietsführer* was looking on to see how well it was performed. As soon as the farewells were over, the Hitler *Jugend* filed out of the hall in a fashion that would have warmed the Lighthouse's heart, if he had had any.

69

As I have told you, the Youth Hostel was an L-shaped building and had a large macadamized courtyard. At ten o'clock this was made brighter than day by the gigantic floodlights that were situated on the roof. At the same moment, ten trumpets blew and drums began beating.

At once, those of us who were in the dining hall, which was on the ground floor, ran up the stairs to our dormitory, from the windows of which we would have a better view.

Column after column of Hitler *Jugend* in perfect formation were marching into the enclosure. There were hundreds of banners, or so it seemed, for each small group of boys had one of their own. The drums kept up a steady beat and the piercing calls of the trumpets broke through again and again, as if they were the voice of war itself, commanding these little soldiers. I looked around at my fellow Danes to see their reactions; I wanted to laugh or make some joke, but I couldn't. Against my will, I was impressed by the spectacle, and I saw my feelings mirrored in the faces around me.

When all the boys had marched into the yard, there was for a moment total silence; then a single trumpet blared, as a uniformed officer followed by his lieutenants made his way in solemn military fashion to the front of the Youth Hostel. Just below the window out of which I was looking they turned to face the drummers and the trumpeters, and the multitude of uniformed youth that stood at attention behind them.

The leader, who was obviously an *Überführer* of great importance, raised his arm and screamed rather than said, *"Heil* Hitler!"

With a deafening sound his *Heil* was returned from several thousand young throats. By chance, I happened to turn toward the next window at the moment. Leaning out of it, his arm outstretched, I saw Pind—the Twig— with an expression of utter bliss on his face.

"Fool!" I snarled.

Suddenly I heard a hundred explosions coming from the courtyard below us.

The drums and trumpets had begun to play again a moment before. Now, in spite of the shouts and screams, they didn't stop, but changed their tempo like a record going around at half-speed. It was all very comical.

The leader leapt into the air and dozens of banners fell with a clatter to the ground. But no one was hurt except in his dignity, which isn't fatal. There was a bit of a scramble while the boys reformed themselves into perfectly straight rows and the banners were picked up; but soon the drums were beating again in their proper rhythm and order had been completely restored.

One of the lieutenants was making his way towards the entrance to the Youth Hostel; foreseeing what might happen, I went looking for Nikolai.

I knew that the explosions had come from some "crackers" that Nikolai had bought. A "cracker" was a tiny little paper bag which contained a minute amount of gunpowder that exploded when it was thrown with any force against a hard surface. Nikolai had bought a whole mark's worth the day before.

I found him and four of our friends in the toilet. The window was wide open and they were standing before it, hysterical with laughter.

71

"This is the first place they are sure to look," I said. "Come on back into the room with the others."

We had only just entered the dormitory when the Lighthouse arrived accompanied by the Hitler *Jugend* officer.

"Attention!" screamed the Lighthouse. His face was so red that it ought to have been visible for several sea-miles.

"*Jawohl!*" screamed Nikolai almost as loudly, though in a slightly higher pitch, while he clicked his heels.

"You . . . You shut up!" shouted the Lighthouse. Nikolai clicked his heels once more and nodded.

"Was it you? Was it you?" The Lighthouse looked as though he might take Nikolai by the throat and throttle him.

Nikolai kept standing at attention, but didn't answer, making it obvious to everyone but the Lighthouse that he was obeying his command and "shutting up."

"Before tomorrow morning, I want whoever did this outrage to report to me. I can only offer my apologies to our German hosts." With these words, the Lighthouse turned to the officer beside him and gave a long speech in German which seemed to satisfy the uniformed man, for he retired from battle and rejoined the parade.

As soon as he was gone, the Lighthouse shouted, "Now who is ready to take responsibility for this disgusting act?"

"It was Twig," an unidentifiable boy whispered loudly.

The misshapen admirer of Hitler screamed in his girlish voice that it wasn't true; but dozens of boys chimed in, all accusing him of being the guilty one.

"I couldn't care less!" Stinker Larsen was standing in

the doorway. "You can all retire for the night now. Tomorrow is another day in which you can make life intolerable for each other, and for the grownups who are so unfortunate as to be forced to be in your company." He cast a quick glance around the room, while the Lighthouse departed; then he stood still.

Nikolai put up his hand and shouted, "Sir!"

The teacher hesitated, no doubt wondering what Nikolai was up to now, but then he nodded in his direction.

"Sir, Mr. Nielson has ordered me to shut up. Is that a temporary order or a permanent one?" Nikolai was still standing at attention.

Stinker Larsen walked over to my friend and glared at him for a long time, as if he were debating some weighty problem within his mind; then the tiniest of smiles appeared on his lips. "Permanent," he said.

9   The Train to Hamburg

"Ich werde warten, bis der Briefträger den Briefkasten geleert hat." Nikolai looked up from the Danish–German phrase book, from which he had been reading aloud. "The correct translation of this gibberish is: 'I shall wait until the postman has emptied the postbox.' The question is, what is *I* about to do? Is he going to murder the postman, but out of his consideration for the general public, has he decided to wait until the poor fellow has performed his duties, or is he merely going to post a letter? In that case would it not be wiser to hurry and put it in the box before the *Briefträger den Briefkasten geleert hat?*"

"Maybe he doesn't want his letter to arrive too early, or maybe he doesn't trust that particular *Briefträger,* but is a personal friend of the one who will collect the mail the following day," I suggested.

We were on the train to Hamburg; the car we were

riding in was not like the Danish ones. It had no compartments, but two long rows of double seats with an aisle separating them.

"It's a fascinating book," Nikolai continued. "It leaves so much to the imagination. Listen to this: *Bitte, warten Sie bis ich meine Schuhe putzen lasse.*" Nikolai grinned. "It is the tail end of a whole novel: 'Please wait until I get my boots polished.' Who is waiting? Why is he waiting? And why is the other fellow polishing his boots?"

"That one is easy . . ." I looked around to see whether either of the teachers was sitting near us. "It is the Lighthouse who is speaking; he wants to kick you, but since he is polishing his boots, he wants you to wait until he is finished."

"I refuse to wait . . . Besides, the Lighthouse doesn't wear boots," Nikolai said and grinned.

Jens, the boy to whom the book belonged, was leaning over Nikolai's shoulder. "But *Schuhe* means shoes. The word for boots is *Stiefel.*"

"Amazing!" Nikolai frowned and pointed to one of the lines on the page of the open book. "There it is— *Schuhe*—and it's translated as boots."

"But that's wrong!" Jens said, so forcefully that neither of us wanted to disagree with him.

"It's worse than wrong, it's terrible!" Nikolai hit his knee with the book. "Such a book is almost like a schoolbook, and when a schoolbook mistakes a shoe for a boot then the end of the world is near."

"It probably is anyway," I said, because I had noticed the Lighthouse making his way down the aisle. I was sitting opposite Jens and Nikolai, and next to me there was an empty place. I closed my eyes and was about to offer up a silent prayer, but I was too late. The Lighthouse had already sat down.

"There is never any excuse for bad behavior," he began without even saying "hello" first.

"They were fascists!" Jens exclaimed excitedly. He was Nikolai's most apt protégé. Nikolai had taught him everything except when to shut up.

Both Nikolai and I looked down at the floor, as if we had, at that very moment, decided to investigate whether we were wearing shoes or boots.

The Lighthouse was bristling with fury. "You should have known before you came here that in Germany you would be guests of the Hitler *Jugend*."

"But we are paying guests, sir," Nikolai replied timidly. "And last night I couldn't sleep because of all the noise they were making."

"How long do you think you would last here, if you were not a Danish boy under the protection of your teachers? Do you think that if you had been German your stupid pranks with the firecrackers would have gone unpunished?"

"No, sir!" Nikolai retorted and even though he was sitting down, he clicked his heels. "I would have had to think up something cleverer, sir; but being only a dumb Dane, I wanted to be found out. I wanted them to know that not all of us applaud everything we see."

"But there are those who do not see everything they applaud, Nikolai," said Stinker Larsen, who had stopped in the aisle. Then turning to the other teacher he asked, "Did you tell them about our visitors?"

"You tell them," the Lighthouse replied irritably. "I'll go and ask some of the others," he added as he stood up.

When he was out of earshot, Stinker Larsen remarked seriously, "I sympathize with your spirit, but don't push your luck too far. You might have got a beating, had the Hitler *Jugend* been let loose on you."

"They would not have been let loose." Nikolai grinned. "They don't want a scandal. Weren't we all invited here to be shown how marvelous the Third Reich is?"

"And you haven't been convinced?" Stinker remarked sarcastically. "Well, I have always said little boys stink and they are stubborn," the teacher said, laughing. "But there is something I must ask you. This morning, just as we were leaving the Youth Hostel in Lübeck, two policemen came to find out if any of us had noticed a strange man on the Danish ferry. They said he was a German smuggler . . . I told them that I had enough trouble looking after my own fifty-two criminals to be bothered about anyone else's."

"What did he look like, sir?" Jens asked enthusiastically, while I turned and looked out of the window.

"They said he was about medium height and was wearing a gray raincoat . . . You can't tell much from that. I wear a gray raincoat myself," Stinker said. Happily, it seemed that he was going to let the matter rest there.

Although I was trembling, I forced myself to look at him; then it was that I noticed that he was carrying a book entitled *Christian Wahnschaffe* by Jakob Wassermann. "Is it any good, sir?" I asked, pointing to it.

"Very romantic . . . I am afraid that I am twenty years too old to appreciate its virtues." The teacher glanced

77

down at the book he held in his hand. "Very German, a twentieth-century young Werther."

"Is it like Goethe?" I asked, proud that I had read *The Sorrows of Young Werther.*

"There are two kinds of Germans: those who are like Bismarck and those who are like Goethe." Stinker Larsen sighed, as he glanced out of the window; we were already in the suburbs of Hamburg. "At present, it is the Bismarcks who rule; but they, too, have read Goethe, and that's the worst of it. I can't say I envy you the world you are going to inherit," he said as he rose from his seat. "I must hurry on to see if any of the other boys have been more observant than you have; the police said they might be in touch with us again."

I was still suffering from the shock of recognizing the title of the book as the name I had been given to use as a password. Nikolai was winking at me; suddenly I remembered that I hadn't told him that I was to say that I was a friend of Christian Wahnschaffe, nor had I mentioned the name of the inn where I was to deliver the package.

"Did you notice anyone suspicious on the ferry?" Nikolai asked.

Jens straightened himself, wrinkled his brow, and scowled. He admired Nikolai and it would have pleased him to be able to say something important, but he couldn't. "Nothing really," he admitted with regret.

"I didn't see anybody either," Nikolai said and looked at me, "nor did Erik. We were too busy planning ways and means of putting the Lighthouse ashore, in case we should happen to pass a desert island. It's a pity we didn't."

Rapidly the train passed over a series of switches, which made it pitch and shake; then it slowed down. We were entering the station at Hamburg.

"He must have talked," I whispered to Nikolai. We had just been herded into a bus which was going to take us to Altona, where the Youth Hostel was.

"But he didn't know your name," Nikolai whispered back, as we took seats in the rear of the bus.

'That's a great help!' I thought to myself sarcastically. All the Gestapo had to do was look through our baggage; when they came to my suitcase, they would find the passports. I would be interrogated and beaten to death.

"I have to find an inn called the Golden Lamb this evening," I whispered as the bus started with a lurch.

"What did you say?" Nikolai asked, because the acceleration of the motor had drowned my words.

"Nothing!" I shouted and turned to look out of the window. It was better that Nikolai did not know where I was going.

The bus stopped near a corner, where two men in black uniforms were talking together. Looking at their faces, I wondered whether they were from the S.S. or the Gestapo. Suddenly one of them noticed the bus filled with boys and waved. I almost waved back. With disgust, I thought, 'You are like a dog that wags its tail as soon as they have stopped beating you.' Then it struck me how silly it all was. I did not even know whether the men in

79

the black uniforms were members of the Gestapo. "Do you know what Gestapo stands for?" I asked Nikolai.

"*Geheime Staatspolizei.* Why?"

"Oh, I don't know . . . No reason in particular." I bit my lip; what I wanted to say was that it would be nice to know the name of your opponent. "*Geheime* means secret, doesn't it?"

"I think you could say the Secret State Police . . . or the State Secret Police." Nikolai grinned at me. "Are you scared?"

I nodded. I was scared. To myself I said, 'I am more like my father than I thought I was. He is not a courageous man, and I am not a brave boy.' Somehow this thought gave me pleasure. I felt all the stronger for having confessed to myself that I was a coward. Aloud I asked Nikolai, "Did you see those two men in black uniforms, where we stopped a little way back?"

"S.S.," Nikolai informed me confidently.

"You know, they waved to us. At least one of them did. It's strange to think that they might have come from beating someone up . . . like the man in the gray raincoat . . . And now they are going home to supper."

"Yes," Nikolai said, and smiled. "Home to kiss their wives and mow the lawn."

"And play with their children," I added.

These thoughts made the world more terrible. Brutes should remain brutes and wear the mark of Cain. They had no business playing with their children or waving cheerfully to a busload of boys.

10 Der gute Wind

The Youth Hostel was a ship!

"It's a three-masted bark!" I shouted, but I had no sooner said it than I wondered whether I was right. But no one disputed my claim, though that may have been because everyone was too busy admiring our new home. Adolf Hitler had never come nearer to converting all of us than during those first few minutes when we climbed on board the old sailing ship, the *Good Wind*.

Most of the standing rigging was still there; only the topmasts were missing. When we were assembled on the deck, the Lighthouse took a position next to the mainmast, and glared at his "crew."

"He reminds me of Captain Bligh," Nikolai mumbled, keeping his hand over his mouth to hide that he was talking.

"Did you say Bligh or Blood?" I whispered loudly.

81

The Lighthouse, peering nearsightedly, finally discovered us. "Silence!" he ordered.

"Aye, aye, sir," Nikolai responded gaily, in true naval fashion.

"I am glad," began the Lighthouse, though he didn't look it, "that some people are enjoying themselves."

A dozen or more boys looked expectantly in Nikolai's direction, but he was mute.

"No one is to climb the masts. It is forbidden!" The Lighthouse tried to look every one of us in the eye at the same time, but he didn't succeed.

Nikolai's hand shot up into the air; with a reluctant nod, the Lighthouse gave him permission to speak. "Can we climb out on the bowsprit?" he asked.

"No!" the Lighthouse screamed, and his face grew as red as the port lantern on a ship.

"Look at that stupid lighthouse," a voice said calmly. It was Jens, Nikolai's friend. What had especially startled me was the word "stupid." The boy was pointing toward the end of the pier, where there was a light on top of a cement pillar in the shape of a miniature lighthouse.

"Could I beg all of you to stop admiring the view and pay attention to me?" Now Stinker Larsen was addressing us. "As you have already been informed, we will have no one playing in the rigging. I must request Nikolai to refrain from his natural—," the teacher paused— "desires, at least until tomorrow, when a visit to the Hagenbeck Zoo is scheduled. I shall then plead with the director for permission for him to visit his brothers and sisters in the monkey cage."

Loud laughter greeted this remark and a low voice mumbled, "Good old Stinker."

"Let me remind you that this is only April; the temperature of the water is at most eight degrees Centigrade. Neither Mr. Nielson nor I am going to run the risk of catching pneumonia by jumping in after some silly boy who has fallen into the sea. Furthermore, may I advise you that the discipline on board a ship is somewhat more rigorous than on shore. The captain can have you keel-hauled or whipped, or if need be, a mutinous crew can be made to choose between walking the plank and being hanged from the yardarm. If you have any questions, please don't bother to ask them, as I don't wish to answer them. Please carry your luggage below with the minimum amount of noise. There you will find bunks, which I hope are as hard and uncomfortable as any to be found in prisons, ancient as well as modern."

"He's great!" There was true admiration in the boy's tone of voice, and a chorus of murmurs echoed his sentiment.

"He is more than great, he is magnificent!" Nikolai plunged his cardboard suitcase down on a bunk.

"The poor old Lighthouse, I did feel sorry for him for a moment there," I said as I threw my valise on the bed above Nikolai's.

Nikolai shrugged his shoulders with contempt. "He's an ass!"

"I know," I agreed, "and that is why I can't help feeling sorry for him. He's like Twig, only grown-up."

"Bourgeois sentimentality." Nikolai grinned. "That is what my father would have said."

"What's wrong with sentimentality?" I asked.

"You mean besides its being good for the handkerchief industry?" Nikolai laughed, but then he stopped abruptly. "The Lighthouse wouldn't feel sorry for me; that is, if he had me where he wanted me."

"I suppose you are right," I mumbled, because I had seen some of Nikolai's friends approaching our bunks, and I did not want to argue with him when they could hear me. Besides, it was true the Lighthouse was mean, and it was certain that if he had had power, he would have misused it.

I climbed the stairs to the deck and leaned out over the railing. "I would rather be sentimental than cold and calculating," I whispered to myself.

It was late afternoon, and lights were being turned on in the distance. Altona was now the harbor of Hamburg and part of the enormous city, but once it had been a separate town. There were no other ships berthed at the same quay as the *Good Wind*. Nearby there were trees. 'It must be a park,' I thought.

"Not exactly the best of places to bring little boys." Stinker Larsen had come up silently behind me. "Over there is St. Pauli, a district filled with beer halls, taverns, and worse . . . It is the most exciting sailors' town ever created. I had no idea that the Youth Hostel would be here."

"But it is a lovely ship, sir."

"I suppose so . . . But again I must be excused because of age . . . Your friend, I have been told, is a Communist. Is that true?"

84

"His parents are." I looked down. A bottle was gently bobbing in the current of the dirty river.

"There are two kinds of Communists: those who want the poor to enjoy the pleasures of the rich, and those who are more interested in making the rich taste the miseries of the poor. Which kind is your friend?"

"He says he is an anarchist, sir. But I think his father belongs to the second group." I smiled, for I could already hear myself using the teacher's wit on Nikolai.

"He is a clever boy. I have noticed him in school. I appreciate a quick mind—there are so few of them . . . I wish I had been born a hundred years ago; that was the time when you could have faith in education. The whole idea of nineteenth-century liberalism was that if the truth were taught, the truth would prevail. We believed—," Stinker Larsen seemed to have forgotten that he did not belong to the last century—"that truth did not need propaganda, that there was no such thing as the good lie. We wanted no more wild ducks, no more life-lies; and we have lived to see the most vicious life-lie ever created." Stinker Larsen sighed. "It is ironic," he began again, "that the country which had the most liberal of all constitutions—for the Weimar Republic had that—should end up with the most barbaric government since man climbed out of the cave, stood up, and declared himself human." Nearby a large neon light appeared. The teacher pointed to it with a grin. "Here and now, I think you are more liable to find truth in advertisement than in politics."

"I don't know much about politics," I said shamefacedly. "I didn't know anything about this—" vaguely I waved my hand—"before I came here."

"And what do you know about it now?" Stinker Larsen's voice sounded almost angry.

"Not much, sir," I said apologetically.

"Neither do I." The teacher let his hand rest for a moment on my shoulder. "Only this: that it is worse, much worse, than we know. It is like an infected sore that has the appearance of being healed, but isn't. Beneath the skin the germs are alive and multiplying. But if you say that to most Danes, they reply that the streets are now clean, the trains are running on time; and then, they tell you about the marvelously cheap vacation they had in Germany."

"We shouldn't be here at all, should we, sir?" I asked nervously, pleased that the teacher was speaking to me, as if I were another grownup, although it made me even more aware of my own ignorance.

"It does not matter." Stinker Larsen frowned. "That is, unless you have caught the disease."

"Oh no!" I said with such fervor that the teacher laughed.

"But," Stinker Larsen held up his finger, "do not go too far in teasing Mr. Nielson. I must uphold his authority as a teacher, if not as a person. You may tell that to your friends. You may also tell Nikolai that I know Mr. Nielson's nickname and—," he paused—"and my own! You can whisper them among yourselves as much as you like, but I do not want to hear them!"

"Yes, sir," I said. I had almost decided to tell Mr. Larsen about the passports and the man in the gray raincoat who had given them to me; but now I couldn't. It was his admonishment, however well earned, that seemed to make this impossible.

"And don't go running around the city by yourself."

I promised that I wouldn't although I was more determined than ever to try to find the Golden Lamb as soon as possible.

There were loud shouts. A group of boys came out on deck; they were playing some kind of game.

Stinker Larsen turned from the railing to watch them. "Without the youth, Hitler would not have succeeded. Never! Yet there are those in our school system who wish us to be taught by the students." He shook his head. "Wisdom is the last of the gods' gifts, and the first one they take away again. Did you ever see a picture of the burning of the books?"

"No, sir," I replied unhappily.

"They were printed in all the newspapers, but I think that no one saw them. There is a type of eye disease that restricts one's field of vision; maybe we are all suffering from it . . . Huge bonfires were made of most of the literature which has made Germany a civilized nation, and around that pyre danced the tailless baboons in their uniforms. There was a big banner on one of the wagons that brought the books for burning. It read: DEUTSCHE STUDENTEN MARSCHIEREN WIDER DEN UNDEUTSCHEN GEIST. Judging from the photograph, most of those students weren't *marschieren* but sitting on their behinds in the truck, tearing to pieces the works of Heinrich and Thomas Mann! They were cleaning the libraries of their country of the un-German spirit, *der undeutsche Geist.*"

Stinker Larsen's voice rose. "That day I decided not to teach German anymore. I decided that as far as I was concerned it was a dead language." Suddenly Stinker Larsen became aware that I was standing next to him, and he probably thought, 'That child thinks me a fool,' for he snorted like a whale surfacing and walked away, leaving me in a state of awe, as though I had witnessed some strange and marvelous feat of nature, like a volcano erupting.

"Have you seen the dining hall?" It was Nikolai, accompanied by Jens.

"No, I haven't," I said, still in a daze.

"It has a great big picture of *der Führer* in a gold frame, but otherwise it is marvelous!"

"I am sure it is," I said.

"Did Stinker bawl you out?" Jens asked.

"No, he didn't . . . Not at all." I looked around; the teacher was nowhere to be seen. "Tell me something, Nikolai, doesn't Stinker teach German in your school anymore?"

"Of course, he does; whatever made you think he didn't?" Nikolai said, laughing.

11   The Golden Lamb

"Bitte, could you tell me where Keblerstrasse is?"

The man to whom I had directed my question had a mustache like Hitler's, but that was the only resemblance. He was blond and little and fat. "First to the right, second to the left. *Heil* Hitler!"

"Heil your mustache!" I said in Danish. It was Nikolai's idea that whenever someone said *"Heil* Hitler," we were to *Heil* back substituting for "Hitler" some absurd word in Danish.

The fat man smiled and said *danke schön,* as if I had paid him a compliment. Usually it was difficult not to laugh or at least smile under such circumstances, but on this occasion, the fact that I was carrying fifty Danish passports distributed among my coat and jacket pockets made it easy for me to keep a straight face.

"First to the right, second to the left," I mumbled to

myself. It was early evening. I had managed to slip out of the Youth Hostel as soon as we finished dinner.

From the fairy tales told to me when I was very young, I knew that every prince who started out on a romantic quest would meet with as much adversity as he could bear before he married the princess and won half the kingdom. Until now I had done none of the heroic deeds that the legends describe; so far I had neither killed a dragon nor scaled a glass mountain.

In my thoughts, I was already in the Golden Lamb; my imagination painted the inn dingy and dark. I saw myself asking to speak to someone and saying that I was a friend of Christian Wahnschaffe. From behind the bar, a peglegged old man winked at me with his good eye—the other was hidden by a black patch. He led me down a dark corridor, and there my fantasy left me. I noticed that there were many people in the street; they were very real and they looked at me too closely for comfort. I returned to Pegleg and that endless, black corridor; and perhaps I should have remained there forever, if I hadn't suddenly seen a sign that said the Golden Lamb.

It was a seaman's tavern, or *Kneipe,* as the Germans call them. Contrary to my imaginings, it was not only clean but rather respectable-looking, the kind of inn a captain or a mate would frequent rather than a deckhand. It had an air of coziness, which I felt as soon as I entered; it appeared to be, in truth, a home away from home to its patrons, a nest to rest in for those seabirds who have flown too far.

A woman who was no longer young, though she was

not old—about the age of my mother, who was thirty-eight—asked me what I wanted.

"Nothing..." I stammered, noting that there was a photo of Hitler on the wall; but then I assured myself that it would be more odd if there weren't any. "I have been told to come here," I whispered.

The woman laughed goodnaturedly, but still looked at me expectantly. "Are you with a ship?" she finally asked, pleasing me immensely by thinking me a cabin boy.

"No." I took a deep breath and again spoke hardly above a whisper. "I am a friend of Christian Wahn-schaffe."

Now I expected her to tell me either to get out or that she had never heard that name before; but she smiled, even more friendly than before, and said, "The captain is not here now, but I will show you where you can wait."

"Thank you," I mumbled in confusion, while I wondered whether there really was such a person as Captain Wahnschaffe. I looked around the room. No one seemed to be taking any notice of me, as if there was nothing strange in a boy my age being in such a place. I was trying to decide whether or not I ought to order something, and if so, what, when the woman pointed to a door behind the bar, and beckoned me to follow her.

It was only a few steps to the door, but when I stood before it, I hesitated. She had already flung it open, and I could see a small hall and a narrow staircase; they were not particularly dismal or in any way unusual, yet I was afraid of walking through that doorway.

"Kommen Sie herein." The woman must have sensed my fear. I smiled timidly and entered. When she closed the door behind her I could smell her perfume; it was strong but not unpleasant.

"I think it is my husband you want to see," she said softly. "Come along." And she started to climb the stairs.

For one moment it occurred to me that I could still turn around and run out of the tavern, and I felt ashamed of myself. 'If I were Nikolai,' I thought, as I mounted the stairs, 'I wouldn't be afraid at all.'

There was wallpaper on the walls of the hall—I can still recall the pattern; it had wildflowers in it. Halfway up the flight of stairs was a window from which there was a view of a tiny yard with a two-wheeled pushcart and barrels piled on top of each other. Even today I think I could draw a picture of that gloomy courtyard, although I only looked at it for a few seconds. One of the shafts of the pushcart was broken, and I can still recall the exact place where the wood had split. Why is it that so often we can remember things which are of no importance whatever and forget the features and faces of people we love?

At the top of the stairs, a corridor ran the length of the house. Its floor was carpet-clad and again there was wallpaper with a floral pattern, this time with red roses.

The woman swung open a door without knocking, as if to say, 'We have no secrets and we do not stand on ceremony.'

"Here, Albert, is a young man who has come to see

you," she announced as she all but pushed me through the doorway.

The room was either an office or a study. Along one of its walls were shelves filled with books, and opposite them, on the other side of the room, were two old-fashioned filing cabinets, flanked by an equally ancient desk. Two chairs completed the furnishings; one was straightbacked and would have served as well in a kitchen; the other was a swivel chair that was being used, though its occupant paid no attention to me. He was bent over the desk writing.

The door closed behind me with a little click, which made me jump, but in no way disturbed Albert, who was now the only other person in the room. He kept on writing, as though he were in a great hurry to finish a letter before the evening post went out. Having contemplated the nape of his neck and his shoulders, which were encased in a black jacket, for several minutes, I cleared my throat.

The man did not raise his head, but he did confess to a knowledge of my existence by saying, "Please wait."

To be told to wait means that there are things in the world more important than you are; it is a way of putting you in your place. As I stood there, I recalled the few times I had been sent by a teacher to the principal's office. There, too, you were made to wait, given time to think of your sins and possibly to repent. You were forced to stand outside the principal's office, thus providing a view of the "bad boy" to everyone who went by. It is a modern version of the stocks, but teachers did not spit on you, as passers-by did on those unfortunates long ago; their faces merely contracted into a severe expression of disapproval or "I told you so." Children, on the other hand, could not help grinning, their features expressing their relief that it was you and not themselves who were standing there waiting for an "interview."

"Well, what can I do for you?" The man swivelled his chair, and the back became the front with a face that had a small pointed beard and two very blue eyes that looked at me through a pince-nez.

"Somebody told me to come and see you . . . I mean to come to the Golden Lamb," I stammered.

"Hmmm." The very sharp blue eyes contemplated me, and then found it necessary to have the lenses through which they were glaring cleaned. The pince-nez was removed and given a lengthy polishing before it was returned to the nose. "Somebody could be anybody."

"Yes," I said. "He was a man in a gray raincoat."

"A very suitable garment for anybody; or indeed, for somebody, as well."

"The police were after him. They arrested him in Warnemünde as he was getting off the ferry." Albert was in no way helpful; it was as if he wanted to make it more difficult for me to tell my story. 'He is like a teacher who is conducting an examination,' I thought.

"And he told you to come here?"

"Yes!" I almost shouted. "That is, after he had given me these." And I grabbed the passports that were in one of my coat pockets and flung them on the desk.

Again, he took off his pince-nez and polished it carefully with his handkerchief; then, while I was pulling out of my pockets the rest of the passports, he studied very intently one from the pile in front of him. "He should have thrown them overboard," he finally said.

"Why?" I asked.

"Because . . . because . . ." With deft hands, he made a stack of the little books, treating them as if they were a deck of cards. "Everything has a value, and the price of secrecy is dearer than that." He pointed to the little store of passports. "However valuable they may be."

"But no one saw them being given to me!" I exclaimed.

"And you told no one that you have received them." The eyes behind the lenses gleamed. I blushed and turned towards the window which overlooked the street; suddenly I could hear the noises of the traffic plainly.

"How many did you tell your adventure to?" Strangely enough, the voice was kinder now.

"Only one," I mumbled, "and he can be trusted." Then suddenly I remembered that I hadn't told Nikolai about the Golden Lamb nor that I was to say that I was a friend of Christian Wahnschaffe. "But he doesn't know about you or about this place. All I told him was that I had been given some passports to deliver; I never told him anything else."

"The password we shall change. I have never liked it —too romantic. Maybe we shall change the place, too." He looked around the room as if he would regret that.

"My teacher was reading the book," I said.

"What book?"

"*Christian Wahnschaffe*," I replied. "He said that he was twenty years too old to appreciate it."

This made the man smile. He was getting up from his chair. And now, for the first time, I realized that he was a dwarf; his legs were as short as a child's. I tried to hide my astonishment.

"You never saw the man in the gray raincoat . . . Yes?"

For a moment I said nothing, then I understood and repeated his yes.

"You never saw me nor my wife." He looked at me earnestly.

"Never," I said loudly.

"And when you walk out of the Golden Lamb, you will forget that there ever was such a place, am I right?" While he was speaking, the dwarf had walked to the door and was opening it for me.

"You are right, I shall forget everything." I smiled and my host held out his hand. In spite of his size, there was plenty of strength in his grasp; but I didn't wince, even though it felt as though he were crushing my fingers.

"*Leben Sie wohl.*" The woman smiled when I returned to the taproom and followed me to the entrance.

"Thank you," I mumbled, and darted out into the street.

Indeed, I felt that I would "live well," or at least, that I would live. Now all thoughts of the police were gone from my mind. It was as if I had just been dismissed from school at the end of the week. No, better still, like the first day of the summer vacation.

I whistled as I walked back to our ship, which shows that I was in high humor, for the truth is that I can't carry a tune, and my whistling is false even to me. My adventure was over; all that was asked of me was to keep quiet until I was home, and then I would have an exciting story to tell.

If there is some devil who has been given the job of spying on those who are too complacent, too smug, how he must have laughed at the sight of that young Danish boy, making his way through the streets of Hamburg, so thoroughly satisfied with himself and his lot. For such a devil would have known what was in store for me, which I didn't.

12 "Twig"

"Did you tell anyone about what happened to us on the ferry?" Nikolai and I were alone on the deck of the ship. Most of the other boys were already in bed.

My friend did not answer right away, which made me sure that he had. "Only Jens," he finally said reluctantly.

"Did you tell him about the passports?" I asked.

"Why do you want to know? Are you worried?" Nikolai leaned over the side of the ship to look down into the water.

"Not really . . . I was only wondering." I did not know why I was asking these questions, for now that the passports were no longer in my possession, it did not really matter. "How many do you think Jens told?"

"No one; at least, he promised me not to . . . But there is someone else who might know."

"Who?" Somehow I knew that the answer would be unpleasant.

"Twig!" Nikolai paused dramatically. "I discovered him rummaging in your suitcase this afternoon. Whether he saw anything or not I don't know, but I think I caught him just after he had opened it."

In my mind, I ran through the possibilities of what Twig might do. He seemed to me the kind who would almost automatically run to tell a teacher; that is, if his parents weren't handy.

"I wonder if he has told Kurt," I said. "It might be just the sort of thing he'd do to curry favor."

"And he would run to the nearest Hitler *Jugend-führer!*" Nikolai hated Kurt so much that he sounded pleased.

"But would Kurt inform?" I mumbled.

Nikolai shrugged his shoulders in a way that meant, 'You're a fool if you think he wouldn't.'

Even though my friend stood beside me, I felt terribly alone. The danger would not be over until I was back in Denmark; but at that moment, it wasn't fear that troubled me, it was something else. "It seems to me that we came here ages ago, not just a few days," I said, trying to express something that I couldn't.

"I haven't enjoyed myself so much in a long time." Nikolai chuckled. "Did you notice that there was a lump of chewing gum on *der Führer*'s nose? It upset the Lighthouse and he took it off."

"I saw it and I thought that it might have been you who had done it." It was miserable standing there talking, and yet feeling as if the person you were talking to hadn't heard you at all. Not that I hadn't experienced this before with my mother—and sometimes with my

99

father, too—but they were parents, and parents hardly ever understand anything.

"It's getting cold," Nikolai said and then added, "but you are not the only one who guessed it was me. The Lighthouse accused me of it and threatened—" Nikolai burst out laughing—"to tell my mother and father!"

"And what did you say?"

"I said that I hadn't even gone near that photograph, and that such a monstrosity shouldn't be hanging in a dining hall; it gave me *Magenschmerzen* to have to look at such a stupid face, especially in the morning before breakfast."

I laughed. "And what did the Lighthouse say to that?"

"Not being very original, he said that he got a stomach-ache from looking at me, which made me say that I was very, very sorry. But I had thought I had a very pretty face because it was Aryan, since I was of pure Nordic blood . . . At that the Lighthouse almost hit me, but he thought better of it and walked away in disgust. Which reminds me—," Nikolai shivered—"that I am going below."

"I'll be there in a minute," I said. I wanted to be alone. Even though we agreed on all the important matters, it seemed to me that Nikolai and I were moving further and further apart. I looked up at the sky. The lights of the city were so bright that only the most brilliant of the stars could be seen. I found the Big Dipper and the North Star.

'It is that he doesn't see how terrible it is,' I thought, 'that's what makes us different. I don't want to put chewing gum on Hitler's nose because that somehow makes him human, makes it all less terrible.'

I walked aft. In the shadow of the cabin, I stopped. On the deck above me, where the great wheel was that had turned the *Good Wind*'s rudder long ago, when the ship still sailed the oceans, was the figure of a boy. Without being seen, I climbed the ladder to the deck to watch him. The wheel had been disconnected from the rest of the steering mechanism and could now be spun around with ease.

Twig wasn't tall, and standing watch by that big wheel made him look even shorter. He was turning the wheel as though he were, in truth, guiding the course of the ship. "Two points to port," I heard him say in his squeaky voice. He was talking to himself, playing, no doubt, both the man on watch and his commanding officer.

Slowly I made my way down the ladderlike stairs. There was something horribly moving in what I had seen. 'If anybody else had seen him, God, how they would have laughed!' I thought. 'But then maybe he's so used to being laughed at that it doesn't hurt anymore ... No, that probably isn't true,' I contradicted myself, 'no one ever gets used to being ridiculed.'

I walked all the way to the bow of the ship. Standing by the bowsprit, I could dream that I was on watch; that wouldn't be absurd, for I was a strong, healthy boy. Had I gone to sea fifty years before, I might have become a gallant foretopman, but not Twig. Dreams are not always lies, but his were.

101

A car swung up onto the pier. I drew myself back into the shadows while it came to a halt by the gangplank. It was only a taxi, and Stinker Larsen stepped out of it. He looked as if he had been grateful to have a whole evening to himself; he had probably dined in town.

Who had I expected it to be? The Gestapo? 'Yes,' I answered myself. 'Well, that's ridiculous. Nothing is going to happen!' And with that thought I went below to my bunk.

In the morning at breakfast, I purposely sat down beside Twig. He did not seem pleased by my company; every time I spoke to him, he answered only yes or no. You can't force anyone to converse with you, so I merely watched him while he ate. His hands were so thin that you could see the bones of his fingers and the blood pulsating beneath the skin. His hair was dark brown and hung in curls over his enormous forehead. Suddenly I wanted to ask him right out what he knew and whether he had talked to anyone else about it. It would have been an absurd thing to do; but as I sat there quietly eating my bread and margarine and oatmeal porridge, I came within a hairsbreadth of doing it.

"Silence! Silence!" The Lighthouse was banging away with a spoon on the side of his coffee cup. "In one hour I want you all to be at the foot of the gangway, where there will be a bus to take us to the Hagenbeck Zoo." The Lighthouse looked around the hall, as if he expected someone to object or disagree. "If you are late, you will

102

be left behind!" With that not very frightening threat, the teacher sat down.

"Are you enjoying the trip?" I asked Twig and almost blushed with embarrassment, because the expression had been such a typically grown-up one. It was something an aunt or an uncle might say to a little child.

"I *was* enjoying it." Twig stared at me as haughtily as he could.

Having been put in my place, I turned from him and sipped a little "coffee." It tasted foul. Whatever it had been made from, it wasn't coffee beans. "Dishwater or bilgewater!" I exclaimed.

"Do you think that the Third Reich should use its hard-earned foreign currency on coffee beans for your pleasure, when there is still so much to be done?" Twig asked indignantly in his high-pitched girlish voice.

"No," I agreed, for certainly I did not expect the Third Reich to cater to my taste in morning beverages, especially as 'there was still so much to be done.'

"Besides, coffee is a drug!" Twig glanced at me angrily. "*Der Führer* does not approve of coffee!"

I almost replied that I didn't approve of *der Führer*; but instead I asked in a most friendly manner, "What is it made from?"

"Roasted barley." Twig took a drink from his own cup, and by heroic self-control managed not to make a face. "You see, coffee has to be imported from America; and the coffee market is controlled by Jews, and they, naturally, won't sell it to Germany except at exorbitant prices."

"I see . . ." I lifted the cup to my lips and gave a tolerable performance of a man drinking without any of the horrible-tasting stuff entering my mouth.

"The whole world is the enemy of the German *Volk.*" Twig pronounced the German word for people or nation, *Volk,* with emphasis. "The other nations are jealous because they know that the Nordic race is superior and ought to be their masters. They will do anything to bring it down and foremost among them are the Jews!"

I nodded, as if I were closely following a lesson and he were my teacher.

"But they will not succeed!" Twig leaned forward and lowered his voice almost to a whisper. "It is not only the Jews one has to watch; there are those who become their tools, and they will be hunted down, too."

"Are your parents Nazis?" I asked.

"My father is a member of the Danish National Socialist Party." Twig's tone told of his pride. "Remember what I have explained to you," he said as he got up.

"I will," I replied and grinned. "*Heil* Hitler to you," I muttered as he walked away. 'He may have seen the passports,' I thought, 'but he hasn't done anything about it yet.'

"Come on." Nikolai was standing behind me.

"Do you realize?" I began eagerly, motioning him to sit down beside me in the empty place which had been Twig's, "Do you realize that Nazi stands for National Socialist?"

"Didn't you know that before?" Nikolai was amazed.

"There are seven depths of realization," I said and

104

laughed. "The *National* had penetrated the seventh layer, but the *Socialist* had not even managed to sink through the first."

As I got up from the table, I looked down and saw Twig's coffee cup; it was still filled almost to the brim with roasted barley water.

13 The Hagenbeck Zoo

Every person has his own particular limitations; the borders beyond which lie the unbearable are not the same for all of us. I disliked intensely being herded anywhere, or marching two by two, or queuing up in a line. The Lighthouse's ambition must have been to become a drill sergeant. He loved rollcalls and took them whenever possible. He counted us as we got into the bus that transported us to the Hagenbeck Zoo, and repeated the performance when we got out. Anyone who could have managed to disappear during the ride must have been a wizard of no mean ability. When he wanted us to line up and be counted before we entered the zoo, all of us objected, even little Twig.

The main portal of the Hagenbeck Zoo was one of those triumphs of bad taste that made one suspect that it had not been designed but was simply constructed from toy blocks by a none-too-bright five-year-old. Two enormous bronze elephant heads, each carrying a street-lamp in its trunk, a polar bear, a lion, and a savage or two are its main decorations.

Once through this monstrosity, several paths were open to us. The Lighthouse charged down one and ordered everyone to follow him. A path to the right seemed more amenable to me, a point of view shared by Nikolai and Peter, who like Jens was one of Nikolai's followers, though he was not quite so docile.

I like visiting the zoo; but I try to avoid seeing certain of the larger animals, like the elephants. In captivity they always appear a bit worse than slightly used. You have the distinct feeling that they are suffering from all sorts of diseases, which make them look moth-eaten before they are stuffed. But most of the smaller animals are pleasant to gaze at and I love to watch the sea lions. No other being has a body so perfectly adapted to its purpose. Oh, to be able to swim like a sea lion! What a pleasure that must be!

The path we had chosen did not lead to any of the great attractions of the Hagenbeck Zoo; we were definitely slumming. Through the bars of a minute enclosure, a melancholy donkey looked at us.

"The door isn't locked," Nikolai observed.

"I wonder what would happen if we opened it," I said, looking up and down the path. No one was in sight.

"He reminds me of Mr. Karlsen," Nikolai remarked, as he flung the gate open. The donkey merely looked at the gap, without moving, as though it didn't care for liberty.

"Old Mr. Karlsen is our Danish and religion teacher,"

Peter explained; he went to the same school as Nikolai. "Karlsen is as bald as the donkey is hairy," he continued matter-of-factly.

"It's their souls that are alike." Nikolai held out his hand and the donkey stetched his neck to sniff it, as though he were hoping for something to eat. "Can't you see the eternal sadness in their eyes, *Dummkopf?*"

"*Dummkopf,* yourself!" Peter walked on. He was easily offended.

Nikolai turned to me. "Should I close it again?"

I shook my head. "Once we have given liberty to someone, why should we take it away?"

"I will *heil* to that!" Nikolai grinned. "But you know, it is funny that he won't come out."

"Remember he is a donkey." We started walking a little faster to catch up with Peter. "But what would you say if someone came in the middle of a math lesson and told you to go home?"

"Nothing, but I'd pack up my books and run for it." Nikolai had stopped in front of yet another small cage, in which a much too large animal of some kind was sitting and, no doubt, dreaming of the jungle or wherever it was it had come from. "Let's open up all the cages," he declared.

"This one is padlocked," I said; and looking at the little metal sign, which was in front of each cage, I tried to pronounce the poor beast's name in Latin, which left me no wiser than the German one had.

"I am sorry I cannot set you free." Nikolai bowed and the bearlike animal yawned. "A pity, you look so intelligent."

108

Someone was gently nudging me from behind. I turned; it was the donkey. "Mr. Karlsen, will you consent to come for a walk with us?" I asked.

"Three donkeys!" Peter, who had an underdeveloped sense of humor, had joined us again.

"Mr. Karlsen . . ." Nikolai was scratching the donkey's head affectionately. "What is your opinion of the political situation?"

"It is unspeakable!" I replied while digging my fingers into the donkey's back.

"Let's take him along to the Lighthouse," Peter suggested. "We will ask him if he is his brother."

"Don't insult Mr. Karlsen," Nikolai said. The donkey had found a bit of grass and was happily gnawing it. "He is too highly intelligent to have such a relative."

"Now look at that fellow." We had turned onto a somewhat broader path, and in the distance, coming towards us, was a uniformed gentleman, flanked by his wife and child. "Why isn't he inside one of the cages?" I continued a little more quietly.

"Where all men in S.A. uniforms belong," Nikolai added.

The man in question had a rather large head that had been set on an enormous body without the convenience of a neck to join the two. His brown uniform was a size too small for him.

"Adolf set him free." Nikolai shook his head sadly. "The doors should have been padlocked but they weren't."

"*Ein Esel!*" The S.A. man pointed to our friend, Mr. Karlsen, who was still following us.

109

"No, it is my brother!" Nikolai put his arm around Mr. Karlsen. But the S.A. man kept insisting that our companion was a donkey and that he should be inside a cage. Obviously it distressed him to find an inmate of the zoo away from what he considered its proper place. He turned for support from his wife and child; they instantly became as indignant as he was, especially the boy, who was a small double of himself in a Hitler *Jugend* uniform.

We went on and the S.A. man followed us. When finally we ran into the Lighthouse and the rest of the boys walking two by two, the stranger appealed to the teacher, as if he were one of the keepers of the zoo.

The Lighthouse sided at once with this uniformed balloon, which hardly surprised us.

"Where does it come from?" he demanded.

"I think it is native," I suggested mildly. "A German donkey, sir."

"What I mean is, where did you pick it up?" the Lighthouse sputtered.

"We didn't, sir; it is too heavy." Nikolai looked surprised. "Would you like us to?" he asked.

"I think, sir," I interrupted, "that one might say that it picked us up."

"No doubt, it thought you were a relative." The Lighthouse's sense of humor was not unlike Peter's— rudimentary. Still, a few of the boys laughed, especially Twig, and the S.A. man's grinning head bobbed up and down with approval. The Lighthouse, out of politeness, had spoken in German.

"I think some people pick up worse friends than we

have." Now I was angry. "Donkeys are nice peaceful animals; at least, we do not associate with jackals, sir!"

"What do you mean! What do you mean!" The Lighthouse was shouting and jumping up and down. He was tired of being opposed, and lost control of himself. Furious, he darted forward and hit me across the face. "That will teach you! That will teach you!" he screamed.

"Nazi!" I sneered. I could feel my cheek growing red and fought to keep back the tears. I don't know what would have happened if Mr. Karlsen had not decided to take part in the argument.

The donkey, wishing to push on, gently pressed his head against the seat of the Lighthouse's trousers and gave him a shove. This unexpected rear attack made the teacher utter an almost ladylike shriek and perform a most ridiculous leap. A roar of laughter greeted his acrobatic effort and I could not help grinning myself.

"What is going on here?" It was a uniformed member of the staff of the zoo, who was followed by the S.A. man's wife and son.

Seeing our friend the donkey, the attendant laughed and said, "What are you doing out, Adolf?" Because everyone else was silent, these words seemed doubly loud.

The S.A. man grunted truculently and glanced down at the swastika on his armband.

"He has always been called that!" The attendant, who was middle-aged, looked around beseechingly at all of us. "He is sixteen years old!"

The S.A. man was not to be mollified so easily; he grunted twice like a gorilla who was about to attack a banana palm.

111

"He is not called after *der Führer!*" The poor attendant looked as unhappy as if he had found himself on the wrong side of the high fence of the lions' cage. Not knowing what else to say, he sprang to attention and shouted, "*Heil* Hitler!"

The S.A. man was not to be outdone, nor was his son, and the *Heil*s rained down upon us. A belated "*Heil* Adolf" came from the perimeter of the crowd, and I recognized Nikolai's voice.

The zoo attendant grasped poor old Adolf's mane firmly and led him away. The S.A. man looked as if he had won some kind of victory; I suppose he had, for I felt certain that the donkey's name would be changed.

The Lighthouse wished the uniformed member of the Master Race good-day, which was an excuse for yet another *Heil* by both father and son.

"I can't stand him anymore," I said to Nikolai, as soon as the two long files of boys were far enough ahead of us so that we could not be overheard.

"I thought he was rather good as a clown; it would be hard to find anyone better." Nikolai was not sympathetic.

"He didn't hit you," I said sourly.

"No, that's right." Nikolai's head bobbed thoughtfully. "I shall get you a decoration: *Wounded on the field of battle and awarded the Teacher's Cross, with Palms and Stars.*"

"You deserve that title more than I do. I heard you *heil*ing poor Adolf," I said laughingly. "Still, in all seriousness, I have had enough of Mr. Nielson."

"As a daily diet, he is rather tiresome," Nikolai agreed.

112

"Old Stinker has the day off. I wonder where he is."

"I don't know, but I wish he were here . . . If the Lighthouse ever touches me again, I'm leaving," I declared with vehemence.

"*Gott mit uns!*" Nikolai's voice harbored both surprise and fear. "Look!"

The lines of boys had stopped walking. Two officers had approached the Lighthouse and saluted him. Their uniforms were black; from where we stood I could not make out whether they belonged to the S.S. or the Gestapo, but they were talking to the teacher.

I looked around. Just behind us, another path had crossed ours. "Tell them I went to the right," I whispered and dashed down the path to the left.

'They have come for me,' I thought; and I knew that I had to try and get away, because I was no hero. Once caught, I would tell everything; and in my mind's eye, I saw the dwarf in the Golden Lamb. 'He was right,' I thought, 'the man in the gray raincoat should never have trusted me.'

14   Alone!

"If you don't stop running, someone is bound to think that you have stolen Hitler's mustache, and start shouting, 'Stop thief!' " I said, trying to be funny in order to cheer myself up. The advice was sound enough; there is no quicker way to attract attention than by running, unless it is to stand on your head and scream.

I came to an abrupt halt in front of the cage of an anteater, but my heart kept beating as fast as it had when my feet were still pounding the ground. I glanced to the right and the left; only innocent visitors to the zoo were in sight.

The anteater is all body and no head, with a very long snout in front. It was pacing back and forth, eagerly awaiting its lunchtime ration of ants. Unexpectedly it stopped directly before me, and opened its mouth just wide enough for its long, thin tongue to shoot out.

"Thank you. The same to you," I said and stuck out my tongue; but the anteater's was longer.

"This is an anteater. It lives in South America." A happy German father beamed as he delivered this information to two very bored-looking children.

"I want an ice-cream cone," said his daughter, casting a fleeting glance at the anteater and deciding that it was not worthy of her attention. She was wearing the uniform of the *Bund Deutscher Mädchen*.

"You have had one already." Her father sounded a little less happy now. "Look at the anteater," he commanded.

"I don't want to. I want another ice-cream cone," the girl whined.

"And I want one, too!" Her brother, who was too young for a uniform, chimed in.

Not wanting to be a spectator to the intimate family scene being enacted in front of me, I walked on. I hoped that the direction I was talking would lead me to the main entrance of the zoo.

Within a few minutes the enormous portal with its absurd sculpture came into view. I was in luck . . . or was I? By walking through that gate and out into the city, I could be making a terrible mistake. Maybe those two officers had merely wanted to ask the direction to the monkey cage. No, they had come after me, and it had been important for them to find me! They had taken the trouble to come all the way to the zoo. Hadn't Stinker Larsen said that the policemen who had spoken to him and the Lighthouse before we left Lübeck had mentioned that they would get in touch with them again in Hamburg?

As I neared the entrance, I noticed that a black car was parked by the curb just beyond it. A uniformed man was sitting in the driver's seat. Automatically I turned back. Could their chauffeur have been told to look out for a medium-sized, tow-headed Danish boy?

Since the ice cream booth was nearby, I went over to it and bought a cone. German ice cream tasted awful; it was only frozen sugar water, just as their whipped cream had nothing to do with cream but was a sticky substance of unknown origin.

"I want a big one!" The girl was not asking but demanding.

"And I want a big one, too!" The younger brother seemed to be made of the same stuff as his sister.

Their father sighed and ordered two of the largest size ice-cream cones. As soon as it was in her hands, the girl began licking it greedily. I thought her tongue was almost as long as the anteater's, and certainly as disgusting.

"Well, shall we go home?" The father smiled pleadingly, first at his daughter and then at his son. The boy's ice cream was dripping down his shirt, which undoubtedly had been put on clean that morning. The girl remained thoughtful for a moment, as she turned over in her mind whether it was worthwhile making another scene for the sake of a third ice-cream cone. At last, she decided to be agreeable—or at least for the present, not to be disagreeable—and nodded.

"Come!" The father led the way and the two children trailed behind him.

116

'If the driver of that car has been told to keep his eyes open for a Danish boy,' I thought quickly, 'then this is my chance.'

Holding the remains of my ice-cream cone in front of my face, I followed directly behind the girl, as if I belonged to that unhappy family.

I was expecting the chauffeur to jump out of the car, machine gun in hand, and scream: "Halt!" But as I passed I saw him out of the corner of my eye, and he seemed half asleep.

Fifty meters down the street the inevitable tragedy happened: the boy dropped his ice-cream cone. For a few seconds, he stood silently staring at the lost sweet, like a mourner before an open grave. Then he screamed!

His sister looked at him with scorn and poked her foot into the slimy mess that once had been so desirable. The father glared at his offspring, as though he desired to commit murder. But he wouldn't, I knew that. He didn't have the backbone that is needed for infanticide.

I gave him a look of sympathy as I went by. Children like his needed a firm hand—if not an iron fist—and he was a jellyfish dressed up as a man.

Walking towards the old part of the city I wondered what to do. I had money, nearly thirty marks; that would be enough for food for several days, so long as I was a little careful. But my clothes were on the *Good Wind* and so was my passport—not that it would have been of much value if the police were looking for me. Indeed, I was probably better off without it.

I passed a store where on display among other items of clothing was the kind of cap that I had seen many boys my age wearing here in Germany. It cost more than three marks, but I bought it because when I saw myself reflected in the mirror, it seemed to me that I looked different.

Now I was less frightened of being recognized; but I still needed a plan. 'If only I could get hold of Nikolai,' I thought as I sauntered down the crowded street. If I waited somewhere near the Youth Hostel I would be certain to see him when they all returned from the zoo; but that wouldn't be until late in the afternoon.

I was so lost in thought that I bumped into someone. *"Entschuldigung,"* I muttered. The man said, "Excuse me," in return without looking up.

Mr. Baumann, our German teacher, had once remarked it was a pity such a "good ear" as mine had been wasted on such a lazy boy; then he had gone on to say something about my learning how to spell, and my moment of glory was gone because I decided that he had just been using modern psychology to make me study a little more. But now I began to hope that he may have meant it. Even though we had been in Germany only a few days, I realized how alike the two languages were; once you get accustomed to hearing German, it becomes quite easy to change a Danish expression into a German one. The words may sound different but in most cases their roots are the same.

It was almost one o'clock. I had to find a place to have lunch. A thing as simple as entering a restaurant and ordering a meal, which no doubt does not jangle the nerves of an adult, can be a gruesome experience for a fourteen-year-old. I stopped in front of more than half a dozen places, but they appeared to me like so many mousetraps.

Finally, I noticed a group of people going down the steps to a small cellar restaurant. I walked in behind them and sat down at a tiny table. A waitress brought me a menu and I mumbled that I would like sausages and potato salad. I lingered over my food as long as I dared, then I ordered coffee. But I couldn't put off forever that awful moment when I had to ask for the bill and the even worse decision of how much to tip. On such occasions you feel so unworthy, so childish; and I was sure that the waitress must have thought me an utter fool, if for no other reason than that I had overtipped her.

For hours I wandered through the streets near the river, but I thought better of going down to the pier, for certainly that would be the one place the police would be looking for me. Finally, I did meet up with Nikolai but it was by pure chance. I had actually given up hope of seeing him when I spied the Lighthouse among a mass of people on one of the broadest and biggest streets in Hamburg.

I made my way in his direction with my head bowed and my hat pulled down almost over my eyes. He was surrounded by boys, but I did not see Nikolai among them. Even the very fleeting glance that I dared cast told me that the Lighthouse was a very unhappy man; but it took me a while to understand the cause of Mr. Nielson's woebegone expression. At first, I thought it might be because of my disappearance.

The solution came in the shape of three boys from my

school, who seemed to have fallen out of step with the rotating earth. They had difficulty standing upright, and propelled themselves, arms around each other, in a staggering manner. They were dead drunk!

"Where is Nikolai?" I asked the oldest of the boys, who had a fine beard of down.

"He is drunk!" The boy's head seemed to be rolling on his shoulders. "He is either drunk or dead!"

At that moment I saw Nikolai and Peter coming towards me. Neither of them looked dead, but they could have been drunk.

"Erik!" Nikolai had recognized me and screamed my name as loud as he could; then correcting himself he put his forefinger in front of his mouth and whispered, "Hush."

"What happened?" I asked.

"We had lunch at a café, where you can get everything out of an automat. You can buy wine, too. You just slip ten pfennigs in the slot, and out comes the wine right into your glass."

"Twenty pfennigs," Peter corrected. "It cost twenty pfennigs for a big glass."

"What happened at the zoo was what I meant," I said with anger and disgust. "I am not the least bit interested in how you got drunk."

"Some of us had got mixed up with criminal elements!" Nikolai nodded. "That's what the Lighthouse said. He wanted anyone who had seen or heard anything strange on the trip, especially on the ferry, to step forward."

"Did anyone?" I asked slowly.

120

"Twig!" Peter sniffed. "The two policemen talked to him and afterwards they asked for you."

"You are wanted by the Gestapo." As Nikolai whispered that name, he put his hand on my shoulder.

I looked around me. "It's not funny," I whispered back.

"Just tell them a lot of lies," Peter suggested.

'What would happen if I told the truth?' I asked myself. 'Told them about the passports and the Golden Lamb?' I was a Danish boy and my father would make no end of fuss. I shook my head as I saw in front of me, not the dwarf from the Golden Lamb, but the Jewish boy we had seen in the alley in Lübeck.

"I'm too scared," I heard myself saying aloud. "I would tell everything, I know I would. I have got to try to get back to Denmark."

"But how will you get across the border?" Nikolai asked as if he suddenly had become sober.

"I'll make it somehow," I replied and shrugged my shoulders, as if I already had a plan. "I'd better go before Kurt and his friends come along. For God's sake, don't tell anyone that you've seen me," I added foolishly; after all, I had already met three of the other Danish boys only a few minutes before.

"What about Stinker Larsen?" Nikolai asked.

"No," I answered firmly. "But in my suitcase, you'll find a little package with a book in it. Please give it to him and tell him to keep it for me." I held out my hand and Nikolai grasped it. "*Farvel* ... good-bye," I said; and then because the word seemed too ominous, I mumbled, "See you soon."

121

"I am sorry I got drunk," Nikolai whispered and grinned. "I've never done it before."

I walked away from them as quickly as I dared without attracting attention to myself. I don't know how far I had gone when I noticed a familiar figure leaning against the wall of an old house.

It was Twig! His face was deadly white. When he recognized me, he gasped like a fish out of water, and tried to straighten himself. The Nazi knife he had bought was hanging from his belt. " 'Blood and Honor!' " I scoffed and took a step toward him.

Frightened, he held up a hand in front of his face to protect himself.

"I wouldn't touch you!" I said, for it had never occurred to me to hit him. Then I noticed a small dark stain spread down one of his trouser legs, to become a tiny stream on the sidewalk. "My God, you little pig! You've dirtied yourself!"

"I'm sick," Twig whined, his eyes growing tearful and glassy.

"You're drunk," I replied. And suddenly I felt that I could do anything, the least of which would be to reach and cross the Danish border.

15 Felix

The great confidence that I had felt at the sight of Twig's disgrace was momentary. After all, the fact that someone else is a fool does not make you into a genius.

It was late afternoon and the streets were crowded. No one seemed to notice me and I did not get the impression that I was being followed; but I knew that night would come, and then what would I do, when everyone who had a home had retired to it? I could not wander the streets; I would have to find a place where I could sleep.

I heard drums. A company of soldiers was marching by. How many there were I can only guess; but the heels of the boots of at least three hundred men hit the asphalt in perfect unison. Each man looked straight ahead as if the neck of the man in front of him held some secret worthy of his attention. Unexpectedly—for no order was given—they broke into song. It was "Die Fahne Hoch";

I had heard it on the evening of "Friendship and Brotherhood" that the Lighthouse had arranged.

"*Wunderbar!*" an elderly man who was standing next to me exclaimed; then because he must have realized that I was a foreigner, he spread out his arms towards the marching men and said, "*Schön!*"

No; although I did not reply aloud, I shook my head. "Beautiful" the soldiers were not. Frightening, yes . . . Possibly even wonderful, in the sense that the sight of these men could fill you with wonder; but never *schön*. The old man did not seem to have noticed that I had disagreed with him. He was staring at the soldiers as if he were witnessing a miracle. A tear ran down his cheek and lost itself in his gray, shaggy mustache.

Had the old man shouted "*Heil* Hitler!" I would have found it reasonable; one could just put it down to the normal behavior of the insane, for everyone in Germany seemed to shout "*Heil* Hitler!" at the least possible pretext. But tears? No, they were indecent. I thought that tear was more than I could bear; I turned from him and walked on.

A black-booted S.S. man was coming towards me. I forced myself to look him in the face as we passed each other. He was young and had a large pimple on his left cheek.

Three young girls dressed in the uniform of the *Bund Deutscher Mädchen* came up from behind me walking arm in arm, and I had to step into the gutter because they obstructed the sidewalk. They were giggling, and the tallest one had green ribbons in her hair. They were followed by two youths of my own age in the brown shirts and shorts of the Hitler *Jugend*. Whatever they were saying to each other, it had nothing to do with politics, and the older boy winked at me when he went by.

Suddenly in the distance, on the opposite side of the street, I spied the dwarf from the Golden Lamb. In spite of the traffic I rushed out into the road and was almost driven down in my eagerness to reach the other side.

I was out of breath when I caught up with the dwarf. He was walking very fast. As I fell into step beside him, he glanced at me for a second, but made no sign of recognition. I was trying to formulate in my mind what I ought to say to him, when my companion stopped abruptly in front of a shop window. I too stood still and stared at the display as if a baby-blue striped shirt were just what I had been looking for all my life.

"The Golden Lamb is finished." The dwarf shook his head. He had said the word *kaputt* so softly that I could barely hear it.

"It wasn't me!" I whispered.

"I know . . ." The dwarf glanced up at me and smiled. "Our mutual friend from the ferry."

I wanted to ask him what had happened to his wife, but I so feared the answer that I didn't. "They are after me now," I mumbled. "Tell me what I should do!"

Anxiously I watched the features of the dwarf reflected in the window. He seemed to be giving my question some serious thought. He was just about to speak when his expression changed to one of horror, as the image of two other persons appeared mirrored in the glass. For a moment we all were motionless, making a strange tableau: the dwarf, myself, and behind us the two men, who, though they were in civilian clothes, bore the mark of their profession as clearly as if they had worn black uniforms.

At the same moment—but happily for me, in opposite directions—the dwarf and I attempted our escapes. As I ran I felt a hand reaching out for me, but it only got hold of my cap and knocked it off my head. I heard someone shout behind me, "Halt!" But I was not going to stop, I was going to run to the end of the world or until I dropped dead.

I did not reach the end of the world, and as you know I am still alive. After I had sprinted a few hundred meters and bumped into a half dozen people, I stopped and looked back. I was not being pursued. It was the dwarf they had been after; those particular two men might not even have known about me.

A clock struck the hour. I listened and counted: One . . . two . . . three . . . four . . . five . . . six. That was dinner time at home. My memory painted a picture of the three of us sitting down to eat, at the long oak table that would have better suited a medieval castle than our modern bungalow. My mother sat at her end and my father at his, while I was lost between them. It was but days since I had left home, but it seemed years ago—almost as though it were a place I had imagined rather than one that actually existed. I shook my head, as if by that action I could obliterate the picture.

"Erik," someone called and I looked around, even

though I knew that Erik is a common name in Germany, and it must be some other Erik that he wanted.

"Are you in trouble?" someone else asked so near me that I jumped.

A boy, a few inches shorter than I, was standing beside me. There was stubble from a beard on his freckled face and I decided that he was older than I was. His eyes and hair were brown. In Hitler's Germany most boys looked like shorn sheep, but his dark hair was longer than my own. Yet what was truly extraordinary about him were his clothes. Here where even postmen resembled soldiers and practically every young person wore some kind of uniform, those who didn't were dressed as unobtrusively as possible; but this boy wasn't. If there is such a thing as the opposite of a uniform, he was wearing it; his clothes were both sloppy and colorful.

"They got your friend," he said sympathetically; then he grinned.

"Who were they?" I asked.

"*Geheime Staatspolizei.*" The youth chuckled, as if the very mentioning of the Gestapo were a cause for amusement, before he asked, "What's your game?"

I shrugged my shoulders as if to say, it doesn't matter what my "game" is. "What will they do to him?" Against my will my voice quavered.

As an answer to my question, the boy drew the edge of his flat hand across his throat; but when he saw my face grow pale, he added, "It depends what he has done . . . Were you changing money? Were you smuggling?"

"Smuggling," I replied in a whisper; and then to my horror, I heard myself saying, "Passports."

The boy raised his eyebrows and took a step backwards to have a better look at me; then he put out his hand. When he grasped mine, he said, "Felix."

"Erik," I replied. "I am from Denmark."

"Dänemark!" Felix drawled out the word, not so much repeating as tasting the name of my native land; then he added that it was a "good country," to which I could not but agree.

"Come with me," he said next and winked. "There is such a draft on this corner that anything may blow down here. Keep close to me, and I will pilot you to a safe berth."

The nautical terms seemed so curiously out of place in Felix's mouth that I felt almost certain that my newly found friend was not a seaman. Yet I followed him as he darted down the first alley we came to, for what else was I to do?

The tall houses left the narrow street in perpetual gloom; from one row of buildings to the other, washing hung like banners. But the lane was a thoroughfare compared to the back streets we now entered.

We walked through a labyrinth for at least a kilometer, then Felix disappeared down the most sliver-like passage of them all. It was less than three feet wide and appeared as a chink among the heavy, dirty walls that surrounded me. The sky became like a ribbon; the air was stale and pungent, as if no wind had ever moved it.

"Welcome to the Cellar!" Felix pronounced *"Keller"* as if there were no other basements in the whole world. With a wave of his hand, he invited me to descend the narrow stone steps.

16   The "Keller"

When an animal finds itself outside the area that it calls
its own, it grows nervous; strange smells attack its nose
and frighten it. It knows that it is trespassing and that
at any moment the rightful owner may begin an assault.
The well-dressed bourgeois who by ill luck gets lost
among the alleys and lanes of the poor experiences the
same fear. As he passes the shabby entrances to the
abodes of those people whom he normally would not notice, he quickens his pace. His imagination populates
these dark caves with lurking criminals ready to rob him
of his money, if not his life.

Some of this fear I felt as I descended the steps of the
Cellar, for certainly I was entering a foreign and strange
world. Yet I had been ejected from the place where I
belonged. I was a refugee from the land of law and order
because it now was owned by Twig and the Lighthouse.

As a fugitive, I had no right to complain of the quality of my sanctuary.

The smell made me wince. The perfume came from several sources, but stale beer and boiled cabbage predominated. The cabbage plant is a humble vegetable, but once cooked it takes on an arrogance which is quite out of keeping with its low price in the marketplace.

Although meals were served, eaten, and paid for there, I don't know whether you could call the *Keller* a restaurant; the title seems to me a little too grand. One might call it a bar or a tavern because wine and beer could be obtained there as well, yet neither word in any way portrays it. A refuge, a retreat, a sanctuary, a safe place, a last resort—together they seem to describe it.

"This is Erik. He may be staying for a while." I looked up to see a huge, shapeless woman stop in front of our table. "And this—" Felix pointed at her as if she were a great distance away—"is the Sow."

I was surprised, but the waitress did not seem to mind her nickname, as if she agreed that it was an accurate, if not a just, description. It struck me as I scrutinized her features that the eyes that looked out from her puffy, doughlike face were not foolish.

"Are you both eating?" she asked in a listless monotone. And although I realized that she probably always spoke that way, I was convinced that she disliked Felix, perhaps it was because she looked at me while she talked to him.

As there was only one item, a formal bill of fare had been dispensed with, along with other such unimportant things as napkins and a tablecloth. The menu was short and to the point: stew! Yet to my amazement, the food was good. The meat was plentiful and not overcooked and stringy, as it had been on the *Good Wind.*

"Who was he?" Felix took a deep swallow from his pottery tankard. One had been placed before each of us, though we had not ordered it, and I assumed that beer came with the meal.

"Who?" I asked and took a sip from my own mug, which until now I had not touched.

"Your friend whom Heinrich's boys took away with them. Who was he?" Felix lit a cigarette and offered me one.

I shook my head. I had tried smoking but I didn't like it. "Heinrich's boys?" I repeated.

"Heinrich Himmler . . . Heini to his friends—not that he has any." Felix grinned in appreciation of his own wit. "Pince-nez Heini, some people call him; but I am sure your friend would call him worse names, though I doubt if he will ever be introduced to the *Reichführer* of the S.S." Felix took a deep drag on his cigarette and blew the smoke in my face. "But maybe he isn't your friend."

I did not know what to call the dwarf; after all, I didn't even know his name. "He is," I finally said, "a friend." But that was mainly because I felt that I would be betraying him if I denied it.

Felix nodded, as if he knew exactly what I meant, and that he, too, had a load of "friends" who were now enjoying the hospitality of "pince-nez Heini."

131

"Did he pay you? Did you get your money?" Felix lowered his voice. "Or did they get him before he had time to?"

It took me several moments to understand what my companion was referring to. Each world—and there are many, and every one is exclusive—has its own morality and its own mode of behavior, which the inhabitants take for granted. Felix spoke like a citizen of the world of criminals, those who trade outside the law.

"You can't always be lucky," I replied evasively.

"Can you get more passports?" Felix's voice was eager.

"In Denmark," I answered, convinced that since I was in the underworld, it was best to act as if I belonged to it; but then realizing that it would be foolish to make too much of myself, I added, "I am just the errand boy, I only deliver them."

"What do they pay you for that?" Felix asked in a businesslike manner, as if he were curious about the wages of a job he was considering applying for.

"A hundred marks a trip," I blurted out before I had time to consider what amount would be right. Felix frowned and I knew that I had made a mistake and grossly underpaid myself. "Plus the price of one passport . . . But they won't pay me that now," I mumbled glumly. "They may never send me again. You know how they are." As I spoke I tried to imagine myself as a small cog in a large machine run by master criminals—the "they" whom I mentioned so often. I tried to picture my chief. What would he look like? The only figure that came to my mind was the peglegged pirate,

Long John Silver from *Treasure Island,* and I grinned.

Several men passed our table and Felix said hello to them. He seemed to know everyone who came to the *Keller,* but he did not seem to be liked by anyone; some did not even bother to return his greeting. There was something about the boy that struck one forcibly as unsavory. It was as if his future could be read too easily in his features. Possibly too, those who, like the Sow, are lost forever, want some innocence to remain in a face as young as Felix's.

Suddenly Felix, who had been slouching on the bench, sat up straight. His expression changed from indolence to alertness.

I was sitting across from him with my back toward the door, so I had to turn to see what had caused this instant alteration in my companion.

A boy who was small and slight and therefore, I guessed, my own age, had entered. I was to learn later that I was wrong; he had lived all of seventeen years.

His pale face was cut in half by a long and very straight nose; his forehead was so high that it looked as if he were already losing his hair. His mouth was small but his lips were very red, as if he were wearing lipstick. He stood at the door surveying the room like an actor making his entrance.

Felix stood up and the newcomer smiled as he slowly took from the breast pocket of his blue blazer a monocle, which he polished in a handkerchief before he screwed it into his right eye. Again he scrutinized the *Keller,* looking from one table to another. Then with out-stretched hand he approached Felix.

My companion beamed as if the handshake had been an honor bestowed upon him; then motioning towards me, he said, "Erik, this is Freiherr von Klein."

17   Freiherr von Klein

As I confessed earlier, you could, without being unjust,
have called me a bit of a snob when I was fourteen. It
was, therefore, not without a certain amount of awe that
I pressed Freiherr von Klein's very soft and somewhat
damp hand. And as I did so, I was wondering exactly
what the title *Freiherr* stood for: Was it as much as a
count or less than a baron?

This young "member of the aristocracy" sat down
next to Felix and with a loud snap of his fingers called
the Sow to wait on him. I couldn't then—and I still
can't—master that art, nor do I know how to whistle
loudly by putting two fingers in my mouth; as a result,
especially when I was young, I was liable to admire the
most worthless people who had acquired either of these
accomplishments.

The Freiherr ordered a bottle of white wine, which
was brought to us together with three glasses. If the Sow

had indicated that she did not like Felix, merely by taking no interest in him, she showed actively her distaste for Freiherr von Klein. First of all, she demanded payment of one mark and eighty pfennigs before she would place the bottle on the table; then when von Klein handed her two marks and told her to keep the change, she refused the tip.

The Freiherr smirked and winked at me. He called the Sow his *Liebchen,* claimed that he was pining away for love of her, and demanded to know when she would marry him.

Shaking her fist at him, the woman declared that she would be his "sweetheart" and marry him next Saturday and bury him on Sunday, if it weren't against her inclination and religion to wring the neck of a worm like him.

This outburst brought appreciative laughter from both the Freiherr and Felix, while I wondered whether I had understood correctly, for how in the world can a worm have a neck?

Freiherr von Klein asked me a lot of questions, very few of which I could answer truthfully. I had to make something up, not because I particularly wanted to, but because I didn't know what else to do. Instinctively, I felt that to explain exactly what had happened, that I was merely a schoolboy who had gotten mixed up in the affair almost accidentally, would be a mistake. At one point the Freiherr accused me of being what he called "a little liar."

"And what if I am?" I said and looked him in the eye.

"Why do I have to tell you things which are no concern of yours?"

"You must do as the Freiherr tells you!" Felix exclaimed menacingly.

'He is a follower,' I thought. 'One of those who attaches himself to another person and like a leech lives on him.' I recalled fights I had had in the schoolyard with boys like Felix who were out to attract notice, and would pick on someone whom they thought they could easily beat. Such battles are hardly worth fighting because there is no glory in winning them. I cast only a fleeting glance at Felix, and kept my gaze on his idol.

"No offense meant," Freiherr von Klein said to me and held up his hand towards Felix like a policeman who is stopping traffic.

"If you ask me what I cannot tell then—" I shrugged my shoulders—"I will lie."

The Freiherr poured wine into my glass and filled his own as well, but gave none to Felix in spite of his glass being empty.

"I like you, Erik!" Freiherr von Klein declared, resting his hand for a moment on mine. "I like you," he repeated and then lifted his glass in a toast. I raised mine and our glasses touched, but I did not declare any love for the Freiherr. In truth, I did not like him at all, and now I wished that I knew of somewhere else to seek refuge.

As I drank the wine, I thought, 'If you don't watch out, you will be as drunk as the Twig.'

"You will stay here for tonight," Freiherr von Klein

137

commanded and did not even wait for me to agree before he called the Sow, by another loud snap of his fingers.

The woman took her time, but she did come. It occurred to me that she not only hated Freiherr von Klein but was also afraid of him.

"You will take care of Erik. He is a friend of mine." Von Klein held up his folded hands to her, as if in prayer. "Give him a bed for the night; I shall pay."

I objected, saying that I would pay for myself, but the Freiherr insisted that I was his guest. The Sow merely nodded as if to say that it was a matter of no importance. She was probably much much younger than she looked. Her skin was smooth and unwrinkled like a young girl's; nonetheless, her obesity made her look middle-aged.

"I must be going," the Freiherr said as he drew a gold watch from his pocket and consulted it. "Five minutes to ten!" He smiled at Felix, who if he had been the kind of dog who had a tail, would have wagged it. "You come with me," he ordered, and then turned to me. "I shall see you tomorrow, Erik . . . *Auf Wiedersehen.*" He got up from the table and bowed as he took my hand; for one horrible moment, I thought he was going to kiss it.

I drew a sigh of relief when I was once more alone. I didn't want to see either the Freiherr or Felix ever again. My glass was still half-filled with wine. 'What will happen now?' I thought as I sipped it. I felt as if I were both watching a play and acting in it. Everything that took place seemed unreal and yet inevitable. 'But isn't all Germany a stage now?' I thought, 'with all the audience rejoicing that for the first time, they are being allowed behind the footlights?' My thoughts pleased me, and I wished that Nikolai were there, for it is not much fun having clever ideas when you have no one to impress with them.

"They call me the Sow," the woman said as she sat down heavily across from me. "But he is really a pig . . . a *Schwein!*"

"You mean Felix?" I replied, although I knew perfectly well whom she meant.

"Freiherr von Klein, he calls himself." She laughed. "He is *klein* . . . small. He is nothing but a rat! As for the other one, the one who brought you here, he is a flea!"

"Is he a Freiherr?" I asked.

"Who knows and who cares; but he might be . . ." The Sow grinned. "Would you like him to be a Freiherr, so that you could go back to Denmark and brag about having met him?"

"What difference could it make to me whether he is a baron or not . . . or a prince for that matter!" I lied. "I was just curious." I was surprised that I could utter such falsehoods without blushing, but then lying is an art that is greatly facilitated by practice.

"I was wrong," the Sow said thoughtfully. "He is not a *Schwein*, nor a rat; he is a spider . . . a fat spider!" It seemed to give her great pleasure to have finally categorized the Freiherr.

"And are you in his net?" I asked, thinking that it would take a fairly strong one to hold her.

"Yes," the woman said, frowning, as if it were a most unpleasant fact, "and so are you." She glanced around the room and remarked as an afterthought, "And every-one else."

"Why?" I asked and unconsciously looked towards the door, as if to say, 'I can walk through that.'

"Come with me." The Sow rose and I followed her.

Beyond the part of the cellar that was used as a bar was another room that was a kitchen and a storage place. In the corner there was a steep flight of stairs. The Sow breathed heavily as she climbed them.

On the landing of the first floor, she paused and sniffed; then with a toss of her head in the direction of an open door, she asked, "Can you tell me what is in there?"

I breathed very deeply through my nose. I needn't have, for the smell was very strong. "Pickled cucumbers," I said.

"Two hundred barrels of them and the floor is rotten. Sometimes I dream that the beams break and we all drown in brine."

We went up another flight of stairs. One single bulb illuminated the dismal scene. The building had probably been a warehouse never meant for living in. At last, we climbed up to the attic, where the space was divided into a series of small lockerlike rooms. Here there was no electricity.

The Sow opened a door, and we were in total darkness until she lit a match. She had a petroleum lamp and when the wick was turned up, the furniture stood out from the shadows. A bed, a bureau, a rolltop desk, and a swivel chair, which seemed outrageously out of place, were the only furnishings. I looked up; there was no ceiling. I could see the eaves—we were directly under the roof—then, as my gaze slid downward, I noticed something hanging on the wall. It was a framed piece of embroidery on which, surrounded by pink roses, the homeland, *die Heimat,* was blessed. The fingers that had produced this work must have long since ceased plying a needle, for the material was so old that it was crumbling at the edges.

The Sow had noticed the direction of my glance. "Yes, this is my homeland." But I could not guess in what sense she meant it. She had sat down in the chair, slid back the top of the desk, and was rummaging among some papers. When she found what she was looking for, she handed it to me.

It was a snapshot, one of those taken by a street photographer. I held it closer to the lamp. I recognized Freiherr von Klein, who was walking arm in arm with someone wearing the uniform of the S.S.

"Who is he?" His eyes were like slits; he reminded me of a pig.

"Reinhard Heydrich is his name, but some people call him *der Henker,* the hangman. I do not know if it is true, but they say that it is he who killed Ernest Röhm."

"And who was he?" I did not try to hide my ignorance though I could see that it amazed the Sow.

"He was another dog," she said and smiled. "He called himself Chief of Staff of the S.A. He is better dead than alive, and so is my husband. Here . . ." The woman handed me another picture, from which several men in uniform stared out at me. "There is Röhm." She pointed to a little fat man with a funny mustache, who looked so foolish that it was hard to believe that he had ever been dangerous. "The man on his right—" the Sow's finger covered a young man with bulging eyes— "was my husband."

"Why were they killed?" The swastikas on the armlets of all the men were plainly visible.

"Who knows ... Dogs will fight dogs." With contempt the woman took both of the photographs from me and threw them back into the desk. "Your friend, Freiherr von Klein, and his friend Felix are both working for the Hangman. He lets me keep the *Keller,* not because he is repentant for having killed my husband, but because it is convenient for him."

Now all that I had wondered at made sense: Felix's jokes about pince-nez Heinrich, his outlandish clothes, even his friendliness, all had been put on to fool some silly idiot like me! Through a small window in the roof I could see the dark night; in a not very brave tone, I said, "I'd better leave."

"You are safer here ... at least for tonight," the Sow assured me.

"What is your name?" I asked.

"Gretl," the fat woman whispered. "But it's all right, you can call me the Sow—everyone else does." She shrugged her shoulders and looked at me defiantly.

"I will call you Gretl," I said.

She sighed and searched again among her papers, and showed me one more photograph. It was of a young girl.

"That is me ten years ago." She laughed. "That is Gretl! Gretl!"

"You were very pretty," I insisted. The picture had been taken at a birthday party or some other occasion of importance. She was staring stiffly into the camera and wearing a long dress, which made it hard to tell whether she had been thin, but certainly then she had not been fat.

"Not really," the woman said, glancing at the photograph as she took it from me. "Come, I will show you where to sleep."

I was led to a room even smaller than hers and much more dismal. There was a bed on which there were blankets but no sheets or pillow. On the seat of the only other piece of furniture, a kitchen chair, stood a half-burned candle. Gretl lit it and gave me a box of matches.

"I must go back down. I'll call you in the morning and then you can decide what to do."

I stood in the doorway while she walked down the long corridor to the stairs, then I turned around to face my garret room.

18   Nobody!

My room was not large enough "to swing a cat in it," as the Danish saying goes; although why anyone would want to swing a cat, I have never understood. Having wrapped the two blankets around myself, I was lying on the bed recalling other equally silly maxims.

One evening while we were having our supper in the Youth Hostel in Lübeck, the Lighthouse and Stinker Larsen had gotten into an argument about proverbs. The Lighthouse had said that they were the wisdom of the people. *"Der Volk,"* I mumbled aloud. "Or is it *die Volk?* Or possibly even *das Volk . . ."* My German was getting quite fluent but hardly grammatical.

Stinker Larsen had disagreed. "I have heard of collective stupidity but never of collective wisdom." Then he had added something about the word *Volk,* or *people,* having been so misused in the twentieth century that he

144

thought it would be a good idea if it didn't cross anyone's lips for the next five hundred years.

Having no pillow I put my hands under my head. I was staring at the strange elongated shadows that my candle threw upon the sloping roof. Much as I tried I could not escape the thought that I was a prisoner here. Suddenly it occurred to me that there might be other people hiding in this loft! My room was not next to Gretl's; hadn't we passed other doors? I sat up and listened.

I could hear the wind blowing softly outside and the scratching of tiny feet, which belonged to mice or rats.

With the end of a matchstick, I loosened the melted wax around the bottom of the candle so that I could lift it off the seat of the chair. I was fully dressed except for my shoes, because somehow I felt safer with my clothes on. In my stocking feet I stood up. What a giant shadow I cast!

As I opened my door a breath of wind blew my candle out. I fumbled for my matches. It was difficult to light one while holding the candle, but finally I succeeded. The little flame banished the darkness around me, but made the depths of the corridor seem doubly black.

The first door I came to was padlocked; nonetheless I put my ear to it. I heard nothing. The next one was also locked and silent; then came Gretl's room and I had reached the end of the hall. I turned and walked back in the opposite direction, trying the doors on the other side as I went along. I could open none of them, nor did I hear anything.

In the room beyond my own, there was a mattress in the corner and I caught just a glimpse of a rat or large mouse scurrying before the light from my candle.

Since I had found no one in any of the other rooms, I grew bold when I came to the last one; and shielding my candle, I kicked the door open after I had lifted the latch.

I stood still on the threshold; there was someone in the room! I cannot tell how I knew—maybe I had heard breathing. Now I could only hear the pounding of my own heart.

I lifted the candle high above my head. In an instant I saw the whole room with its table, chair, and small closet; but my attention was caught by the bed, for underneath the blankets I could clearly distinguish the figure of a person. My first thought was to go away and close the door behind me; but I realized that the lumps were too small to be made by a grownup, unless he was a midget or someone very old.

"*Guten Tag* . . . Good-day," I said, which was a little absurd, since it was the middle of the night.

The bulges beneath the bedclothes moved, but did not answer.

I reached out and lifted a corner of the blanket. A fringe of black curls became visible. I drew it back a little further and saw two frightened eyes; and at last the face of a girl my own age emerged.

"Who are you?" I asked, unable to hide my relief at finding someone that I need not be afraid of.

"*Niemand* . . . Nobody," the girl answered in a whisper.

146

I smiled encouragingly. "My name is Erik Hansen. I am a Dane." I waited and when the girl remained silent, I added, "I am hiding here."

She just stared at me. Her eyes were brown; in the dim light their pupils were large and very black. "I am staying in a room further up," I said and pointed towards the wall. "Gretl brought me here."

"Yes," the girl mumbled, but she said nothing more.

"I'm from Copenhagen. Do you live here?" I asked, looking around the tiny room.

"Yes," she whispered, watching me like a bird who is ready to fly. "It was very cold this winter."

"You mean you live here all the time?"

"I came here a year ago . . . I remember, it was a week before my birthday." She wrinkled her brow as if she wanted to recall something that had escaped her. "And that was just before the Easter vacation, when I was taken out of school."

"You don't go to school?" I asked unbelievingly.

"No." She shook her head. "Not any more. Just before Easter my mother said I would get a new father."

"A new father?" I echoed in confusion.

"But I couldn't." The girl folded her hands. "You see, my father is dead. But my mother changed her mind and said I couldn't have a new father . . . Instead I had to come here."

I hoped the girl could not see in my face that I was wondering whether she might be crazy.

"You see . . ." She put her hand up to her mouth and bit it; for a moment, it appeared as if she were going to cry, but she didn't. "My father was a Jew. You see, my

147

mother was not allowed to marry him, except she hadn't known that, when she did it." The girl paused as though what she was saying was something she had never expressed before. "But I liked my father . . . He was very nice. But he didn't like Hitler." She looked up at me, and then continued as if she were teaching a lesson. "You see, here in Germany, we all have to like Hitler."

"I don't," I said.

"But everyone else does. When I was in school, they all did except one boy; and they took him out of school." Suddenly she added with pride, "I went to a private school."

"What happened to the boy?" I asked.

"I don't know; he left before Christmas. All the Jews left. I don't know how many there were, but he was the only one in my class." She looked very confused; then she remarked quietly, "You see, I am not a real Jew . . . that's what my mother said . . . That is why I stayed in school till Easter."

"But your father was a Jew," I said softly.

The girl nodded. "But that doesn't matter. It is only your mother that is important." For the second time the girl brought her hand up to her mouth and bit it. "But that is not true either, for, you see, she couldn't keep me . . . I am just *Niemand* . . . nobody! Nobody!"

"Does your mother come to see you?" I asked.

"Once." The girl sniffled but she did not cry. "She came once; but you see, she couldn't come again . . . not here." The child looked around her attic cell. "And I am not allowed to go out."

"You mean you never get outside?" I asked in wonder. "You have to stay here all the time?"

"Sometimes Gretl takes me down to her room, when there is no one else up here. But most of the time I stay right here."

"But nobody," I protested, "could live here all the time and never go outside."

"Oh, yes." The girl smiled faintly. *"Niemand* . . . nobody can."

"So you found her!" a voice said from the darkness of the corridor.

I turned. Dimly I could see Gretl, and I wondered how long she had been standing there.

19   I Get a Traveling Companion

"She is my niece, my sister's daughter." Gretl looked at the girl as though she were perusing her features to see whether she resembled that sister. "Come along, the both of you, down to my room."

We obeyed and the three of us filed down the corridor: Gretl first, then the girl, and finally myself carrying the candle.

In the light of Gretl's petroleum lamp, I saw Nobody clearly for the first time. Her face was so unnaturally pale that I readily believed that she had not been outside the garret for a year. 'But she is pretty,' I thought. Her curly hair was shoulder-length and her features were fine and delicate; then I noticed that her dress was much too short for her and in a style more fitting for a younger child. It was obviously something that had been bought a long time ago.

"Sit down." Gretl pointed to her bed, while she herself sat down in the swivel chair, her enormous hips bulging at the sides of it.

"Everyone told my sister that she was a fool when she married a violinist and a Jew on top of it!" Gretl shook her head, as if she were once more arguing with her sister. "What good could come of it?"

"But he is dead," the girl said softly.

"And one doesn't speak badly of the dead! Why not?" Gretl sniffed. "Your father was not a bad man; he could not help that he was a Jew. But my husband was bad, and I won't forget that! No, never!"

It struck me that Gretl was drunk, but that did not keep me from asking, "What had your husband done?"

"Killed more men than you have fingers and toes," she answered and tossed her head.

'Isn't there pride in her voice?' I thought.

"But that was not the worst of it," she continued without looking at me. "It was his pleasure in it. He would brag about it, as other men brag about all the women they have loved."

Quickly I glanced at the girl; besides being a bit of a snob, I was a puritan as well. Nobody was sitting contemplating her feet, as if she had heard nothing unusual.

"Wasn't he in the S.A.?" I asked, remembering the photograph Gretl had shown me earlier.

"From the very beginning. *Sturmabteilung* . . . storm troopers." Gretl smiled sarcastically. "Before that he had been in jail . . . But I didn't know that."

"Why did you marry him?" I asked before I realized what I was saying.

The woman shrugged her shoulders. "Why does anyone marry? Because he asked me. I was never beautiful. He was very big and strong. He used to call the S.A. *Freude durch Kraft,* 'Joy through Strength.' It was a joke of his." Her glazed, bloodshot eyes rested on me. "You must have heard of *Kraft durch Freude* ... 'Strength through Joy'?"

"But I haven't," I replied apologetically.

"They arrange your holiday. It is run by that drunkard, Robert Ley." Gretl snorted; then she was silent for several moments. When she began speaking again, it was as if she had not paused at all. "Werner used to say that he got as much pleasure out of smashing a man's head like a coconut as he would out of a two week's cruise on one of Ley's boats. He used to beat me, and he was the first one to call me the Sow."

Again, it seemed to me that I detected pride rather than shame in Gretl's voice. The young girl was still contemplating her toes, and I realized that Gretl was probably often drunk and that Nobody had heard all this many times before.

"Well, they smashed his head ... Heini's boys." She sighed. Suddenly she noticed her niece and said irritably, "Isolde, sit up straight. You need some new clothes."

"Niemand!" The girl insisted. *"Niemand!* Nobody!"

"My sister was very fond of Wagner. If she had had a son, she would have called him Tristan." Gretl grinned. "I don't like Wagner, I like Strauss. Johann Strauss. I love to waltz. Do you like to dance?"

"Not particularly," I replied, fearful that in the next

breath she was going to ask me to dance with her. "But I don't like Wagner either."

"My name is not Isolde! My name is Niemand . . . Nobody." The girl was looking at me. "Don't ever call me by that name; that belonged to another girl who lived with her mother. Remember that my name is Nobody. If you don't, I won't ever talk to you again," she added childishly.

"I will remember." I caught her glance and looked straight into her eyes. "I will only call you what you want me to," I said seriously.

The girl smiled.

"Do you like Erik?" Gretl asked the girl. When Nobody both nodded and blushed, the fat woman laughed loudly. "That is good because he is going to take you to Denmark . . . Dänemark is filled with butter and cream. There they feed little girls on cakes."

I looked at Gretl and then at the girl. Somehow I was not surprised that I had been given a part in this play; it was as if I had expected it. "I will take her," I said, though it was ridiculous, because I had no idea how I was going to escape myself.

"She can't stay here any longer. The Freiherr von Klein knows she is here and if he knows then the Gestapo knows . . . She is no longer safe."

"Are you sure?" I asked. What I really wanted to say was, 'Are you certain that it is not your own safety you are worrying about?'

"The Freiherr is always poking his long nose into every crack." Gretl's eyes narrowed. "He also knows who her father was and who her mother is now married to."

153

I frowned, trying to understand the laws that governed this strange world that chance had dropped me into.

"She is married to an S.S. *Obergruppenführer*." Gretl crossed her arms and waited for this important piece of information to make its impression.

"And how does that matter?" I asked.

"Matter!" Gretl laughed unpleasantly. "An *Obergruppenführer* is like a general in the army. What do you think *der Führer* would say if he knew that such a man was married to a woman who had once been married to a Jew and had even had a child by him?"

"I wouldn't know and I wouldn't care!" I said angrily. Nobody was staring at me, her face as white as chalk. "You will come with me to Denmark, and we shall feed you on whipped cream cakes." I smiled but the girl did not smile back.

"Now you know why she must be gotten out. So long as she is alive, the *Obergruppenführer* will not feel safe!"

I felt like saying, 'And neither will you nor your sister.' But I didn't because this would only pain the girl. 'What kind of mother can leave a child she has given birth to?' I asked myself.

"When you get to Denmark, you can be Isolde again." Gretl had turned to Nobody, but the girl looked away. "There no one will mind that your father was a Jew."

With sudden pain, I recalled at that moment that this wasn't altogether true. I had an uncle, my mother's brother, who often made nasty remarks about Jews. He was a fat, jovial man, but very stupid, and my father didn't like him.

"Isolde is dead. Don't ever mention her name." The

154

girl's voice was low and furious. "They killed her," she said with passion, without telling us whom she meant by "they."

"Tomorrow ... I'll tell you my plans, tomorrow." Gretl yawned as a sign of dismissal.

I took my candle; the girl followed me as if she were already in my charge. I led her to her room and watched while she climbed underneath the blankets.

Just as I was going to bid her good-night, she said, "Sometimes a father is not your father. I have heard of that." She hesitated. "But your mother is always your mother, isn't she? There can't be a mistake, just as with a father?"

She had turned her back towards me and her face to the wall.

"Oh, sometimes I suppose there could be," I replied, not very convincingly; then I remembered that I had heard of a case in Denmark where two babies had been exchanged in the hospital, and told her about it.

"Then I wouldn't be me at all!" She sat up and looked at me, then for the first time I heard her laugh. "No, I wouldn't like that at all. It wouldn't be fair to that poor other girl who would be me."

I grinned. "Whatever we are, we are; and maybe it is the best, though I have often wanted to be someone else."

"You have!" the girl exclaimed incredulously. "Who?"

"I don't know ... Just someone else," I lied, for in truth, when I had had such fantasies, I was always at least a count and sometimes a prince.

"Maybe everybody has dreams like that." She lay down again. "Maybe no one wants to be who they are."

155

"Maybe," I agreed, although I did not feel certain that this was true. Surely, there were some people who were satisfied with themselves. "Good-night," I said, then I whispered the name she had given herself, "Nobody."

"Good-night." She too paused before she said my name, "Erik."

Just as I was about to close the door, her little voice asked from beneath the blankets, "How old are you?"

"Fourteen," I answered and asked, "And how old are you?"

"Thirteen," she replied. "Good-night."

20 Erik's New Clothes

I should have closed the door to my garret room more quickly, for enough doubt, fear, and panic sneaked in with me to keep me awake long into the night.

As I climbed into bed, I said to myself, "I am not afraid." But though I repeated these brave words several times, they didn't seem to bolster my confidence. Finally, I thought, as I lay there listening to the scampering feet of the rats and mice, 'Better to be honest: I am afraid, I am petrified, I am a coward!' I put my head under the covers and mumbled these magic phrases a few times. I felt much better and a little less scared.

Gretl woke me in the morning to tell me that Freiherr von Klein was asking for me. I told her that I did not wish to see him ever again, but Gretl insisted that I had to. Her hair was neatly combed and she looked surprisingly alert, considering how drunk she had been the night before.

Slowly all the unbelievable things that had happened fell into place in my mind. "Now that I know that he is a Nazi, it will be very difficult for me to be polite to him."

"But you will be!" Gretl looked at me seriously. "I have a plan for you and my niece, and you wouldn't want to spoil it, even for your own sake." Suddenly she laughed. "You'll do everything I tell you. I know you will because you're a good boy."

I sat up in bed. 'How shocked my mother would be to know that I slept with all my clothes on,' I thought; then I too laughed. "Yes, I am a good boy," I said.

Gretl was standing in the doorway, which her huge body almost filled. "You must let the Freiherr believe that you are staying on here. You must not tell him anything else! Nothing, do you understand?"

"I wouldn't tell him the right time, even if I knew it," I replied, looking at my pocket watch, which I had placed on the seat of the chair before I went to bed. It had stopped; I had forgotten to wind it.

"It is ten minutes to nine." Gretl's wristwatch was one of those very tiny ones that are very expensive. "Come down—Freiherr von Klein doesn't like to wait."

"All right," I said and swung out my legs. With my feet I groped for my shoes while I wound my watch and set it.

"If you want to wash, you can come to the kitchen first." With those words Gretl left.

I sighed and tied my shoes. This was the first morning in my life that I had not put on clean underwear and socks. 'Maybe my feet will fall off,' I thought and grinned.

158

In the corner of the kitchen was a sink. I washed my face under the cold-water tap; there was no hot one. Gretl gave me a towel, which, only too obviously, I was not the first person to use. I combed my hair, but I had no toothbrush. My morning toilet was quickly completed.

I was very glad to see that Freiherr von Klein was alone. "Good morning," I said.

He lifted his behind exactly five inches above the bench, while shaking my hand; then he seated himself again and beckoned me to sit opposite him. We were occupying the same table as we had the night before.

"Have you slept well?" he asked.

"Very well," I lied.

"You were not disturbed . . ." (the Freiherr smiled expectantly) "by any of the other guests in the . . ." (again he paused, as if he could not find the correct word) ". . . hotel?" he finally uttered.

"I thought I was the only one there," I said, pretending to be surprised. "I didn't hear anybody, unless you are referring to the rats and mice."

"Hardly." Freiherr von Klein grimaced. "I hope you did not have to share your bed with them. No, I was thinking of much more attractive vermin."

"What do you mean?" I asked, hoping that my face resembled a question mark.

"A girl." He lowered his voice to a whisper. "The Sow keeps girls up there . . . Jewish girls."

"Are you sure?" I asked.

"Yes, I'm sure; you can tell the Sow that." The Freiherr kept his gaze on me as if he were trying to hypnotize me.

159

"Why don't you tell her yourself?" I replied as casually as I could. "It has nothing to do with me."

The Freiherr laughed. "Haven't you noticed that she hates me?"

"Why should she?" I demanded, while to myself I thought that I could easily give twenty-six and a half good reasons why I hated him.

"Envy, I suppose." The Freiherr yawned as if the subject bored him. "She is filled with the envy of the proletarian for the aristocrat. Haven't you ever felt it being directed against yourself?"

The compliment was very deliberate; and though I was a snob, I was not quite that stupid. "I am not a nobleman," I said, and managed to look as if I were not ashamed of that fact.

"She is the scum . . . the rabble." The Freiherr's voice was so filled with hate that even he was embarrassed by it. "She belongs to the vulgar herd," he said, returning to his usual bored tone. "I believe she has a good heart," he added, in this way admitting that compassion was not the property of a single class. "The Sow is harmless enough. She can even be useful, when she wants to be. It is just my fastidiousness . . . She offends my delicate esthetic sense." The Freiherr's smile erupted into a chuckle.

"She is awfully fat," I admitted.

"There is a great deal of coarseness in our modern age —a savage barbarism which, though attractive in some ways, repels me in others." The Freiherr gently rubbed his hands together. "You know that she is well connected."

160

I shook my head.

"Oh yes, her husband was a friend of Röhm, the leader of the S.A. They both had to be eliminated." He pronounced the word syllable by syllable. "She has even known *der Führer*." The Freiherr looked at me intently, to see how I would react to this news.

"You mean she is a Nazi?" I exclaimed, acting amazed.

Freiherr von Klein looked puzzled, as if he were thinking that even to my naiveté there must be limits. "She was one of the first Nazis." The Freiherr bit his lip and then leaned forward. "I think she still is loyal to *der Führer,* but . . ." Now he whispered. "I am not sure whom she is working for. Even within the party there are factions. The fat one would love to know about that girl."

"The fat one?" I was so thoroughly confused that I thought I might have misunderstood him.

"The *Reichsmarschall* Hermann Göring, who has no love for Heinrich Himmler, the *Reichsführer* of the S.S.," he said slowly.

'If they are like dogs fighting each other, then the Freiherr is a poodle,' I thought. "But if she is a Nazi," I said aloud, "why should she help a Jewish girl?"

"She has her reasons . . . Besides, the girl is her niece." The Freiherr looked grim. "Listen, make sure that girl is still here and keep your eyes open. If you play my game, I shall play yours and get you back to Denmark."

"Yes," I promised, though what I wanted to say was, 'And what will happen if I don't?' But somehow, I felt that I didn't need to.

The Freiherr seemed to have guessed what I was

thinking, for as he rose from his chair, he said, "I am fond of you, Erik. I would hate to see anything happen to you. It would be a shame."

"What did he want?" Gretl asked as she placed before me a cup of coffee and a roll with a thin slice of cheese.

"He said that he was so fond of me that he would burst into tears if anything happened to me." To my great surprise the coffee was real.

"Didn't he ask you about my niece?"

"Yes," I said, but did not look at her. I took a bite of the roll and chewed it slowly. I didn't know how much I trusted Gretl. "He also told me that you were a Nazi." I raised my glance to hers. "Is that true?"

Gretl laughed. "If I were, I would lie about it to you; so it doesn't matter what I say . . . But now you will believe that my niece is no longer safe here, and that she must be gotten out of the country?"

I wondered whose safety Gretl was concerned about, the girl's or her own. "The Freiherr said he would come back tomorrow."

"By that time you will be gone. You might even be in Denmark . . ." She noticed my empty cup and offered me more coffee. "It's real," she boasted, as she poured it. "I am going now; I shall be back soon."

"What if someone comes?" I asked, waving my hand towards the dozen or so empty tables and benches.

"I shall lock the door. If anyone knocks, don't answer."

"Where are you going?" I demanded.

"To buy two tickets to Flensburg. From there on you

must make it on your own," she said, as she put on her black leather coat.

"Flensburg is the border; we'll make it across all right," I replied happily. I believed it because I was so relieved that soon we would be away from the *Keller* and Freiherr von Klein.

"Stand up," Gretl ordered. I obeyed but at the same time demanded to know why. "So that I know what size to buy your disguise," she answered when she reached the door.

Twice while Gretl was away someone tried the handle of the door, and on the second occasion it was followed by a loud knock. I hoped that it was neither Freiherr von Klein nor his friend Felix, because they might be suspicious if they found the place locked.

I drank the rest of the coffee that was in the pot; and then, because I had nothing else to do, I washed the dirty dishes in the kitchen and swept the floor both there and in the bar. This kept me quite busy, as no one had straightened up from the night before, and I was surprised that more than an hour and a half had gone by when Gretl returned.

"You see, I was right, you are a good boy!" she exclaimed, as she deposited some packages on the kitchen table.

I blushed and wished to God that I had done nothing. "I was bored," I explained as an excuse for all my efforts.

"When good boys are bored they sweep floors, when bad boys are bored they dirty them. That is the difference between good and bad boys!" Gretl had a knife in her hand and was cutting the string around one of her

163

packages. "As a special reward, I have a gift for you." Deftly, she unwrapped the box. Then she held up the items one by one for me to inspect: the brown shirt, the black shorts, the belt, the shoulderstrap and the scarf. All the parts that together made up a Hitler *Jugend* uniform.

21 We Leave

"I won't wear it." Nobody looked at me while she shook her head from side to side.

"Do you think I want to wear this?" I pointed to the Hitler Youth uniform that I had finally and most reluctantly put on.

"They killed my father!" The girl threw the blue-pleated skirt of the *Bund Deutscher Mädchen* across the bed.

"I know . . . But you don't understand, they won't expect us to wear this. It is a disguise, like something you wear at a masquerade."

"What is a masquerade?" Nobody frowned.

"It's a fancy-dress party. You dress up as anything you like. I had one for my fourteenth birthday. Don't you have them here in Germany?"

"I have never been to any parties," Nobody said softly, as if she doubted the truth of what I was telling her.

"It was all my mother's idea," I said, feeling as stupid now as I had then. "She wanted me to dress up as an Indian."

"And what did you dress up as?"

"A pirate," I answered. "There were six Indians at the party, three cowboys, and four pirates."

"Well, that's fine. We will dress up as pirates. They won't expect that either." Nobody picked up the white blouse of the League of German Girls' uniform between two fingers and dropped it on top of the skirt.

"Don't be silly," I said, rather exasperated. I was learning that Nobody was not only very clever but that she had a fine sense of humor. "Now put that uniform on!"

"There you are!" she exclaimed, taking the scarf and arranging it like a kerchief around her head. "You have only had the Hitler *Jugend* uniform on for ten minutes, and already you are a bully."

"I am not a bully," I sighed and sat down on the bed beside her. "The dress you are wearing is much too small for you. If you wore that everyone would look at you, and that is the last thing we want. You only have to wear this—" I pointed to the uniform—"until we get to Flensburg. As a matter of fact, in Denmark you would not be allowed to wear it. It is against the law to wear any uniform but the Scouts'."

"You mean that in Denmark, the police will prohibit you from wearing a Hitler Youth uniform?" Nobody asked. I nodded. "I think I shall like Denmark," she said and smiled.

"Then please," I pleaded, "put on that uniform for my sake!"

"For your sake." Nobody laughed. "So that we will match each other?" she asked.

"Yes," I replied, "so that we will match each other."

"All right, I will do it." The girl started to unbutton her dress. "You go down to the kitchen and wait."

"Take your dress with you," I said. "I will have a knapsack; you will want to change into it once we are in Denmark."

"But it is too short," Nobody said, teasing me.

"It will do until you find something better. My mother will buy you a dress," I said.

"What is your mother like?" The girl grew suddenly serious.

"I will tell you later." Her questions were beginning to irritate me. "We have to catch a train."

"And you have a father, too." Again the girl was teasing me. "Nobody has neither a father nor a mother, but everyone else has one of each. I don't think I shall call you Erik. I shall call you *Jedermann* . . . Everyone. Then we shall really match each other—Jedermann and Niemand—Everybody and Nobody."

"I don't care what you call me as long as you get ready to go." With these words, I turned my back on the girl and went down to the kitchen.

"How long has she called herself Nobody?" I asked. "After all, she does have a perfectly good name."

"Is Isolde a perfectly good name for a Jew?" Gretl

asked impatiently, as she wrapped the sandwiches we were to take with us in brown paper.

"She is only half a Jew," I said defensively.

"Oh, they are large about it; half a Jew or even a quarter is as good as a whole one," Gretl said, while she continued packing our food in a cardboard box that once had contained cubed sugar.

"What would they do if they caught her?" I asked.

"That won't happen," Gretl replied.

"But what if it does?"

I knew what I wanted her to say, that no harm would come to the girl, but Gretl remained silent until she had finished preparing the food for our journey.

"I tried to persuade my sister to find some way of getting Isolde out," she began in a monotone. "But she could not or would not. Do you think I would ask a child like you for help, if there were anyone else? One day I even tried to approach an American tourist. Isolde has an uncle in America—" she hesitated—"a Jew. But I don't know his address. I told the American all I knew about him and asked him if there wasn't some way we could find out where he lived, and if he wouldn't help. Do you know what that American did?"

I shook my head. How could I know?

"He stuck a ten-mark bill into my hand and said he was sorry, but he couldn't do anything illegal."

"Everyone looks out for himself, I suppose," I said foolishly.

"Here." Gretl handed me a large white envelope. "Inside you will find her birth certificate and the name of her uncle . . . I think he used to live in New York City, but I am not sure. There is a hundred marks in there. You can use some of the money if you need to, but I meant it for her."

The envelope felt quite bulky. "I think I have enough money of my own," I said quietly. "Besides, if I had to use any, my father would always repay it."

Gretl smiled. "Here are the two tickets to Flensburg —now don't lose them. The train leaves in an hour."

"Are you satisfied? Do I look the way you want me to?"

Neither Gretl nor I had noticed the girl coming down the stairs. Now she turned around so we could inspect her. Nobody had done her best. Her hair hung in pigtails. Yet she still looked more like someone who had just risen from a sickbed than an ideal member of the *Bund Deutscher Mädchen*.

"You look fine," I said and smiled. "Give me your dress." I opened the knapsack and put it in together with the envelope. "If anyone asks you, just say we are brother and sister."

"And how do I explain that my brother speaks German like a parrot?"

"I don't speak German like a parrot," I protested. I was rather proud of my accent.

"You do, too!" the girl insisted. "I shall tell them that you are my cousin from Dänemark, and in Dänemark they feed little boys on cream and that's why you are so fat."

"I am not fat!" I was beginning to realize that travel with Nobody was not going to be easy.

"You sound as if you were brother and sister." Gretl

169

laughed; but then, looking at her watch, she became serious. "You must take the train that leaves at ten minutes past twelve. It is a slow train and you must change at Kiel; but it will be safer than an express train, because you would expect people who were fleeing to be on the fastest train they could get. It will take you about a half an hour to walk to the station. Isolde knows the way."

I stood up and put the knapsack on my back. I was ready.

"I will go first," Gretl said when we entered the tap-room, which was still closed to customers. "I'll wave to you from the end of the alley; then you'll both come."

She unlocked the door, but before she opened it, she turned to Nobody. "I have done my very best for you," she said, almost pleading.

Somehow, when I heard her say it, I felt certain that she hadn't. What chance did we really have to get across the border? She was trusting her niece to a fourteen-year-old boy. For one moment only, I realized the absurdity of the situation; then my pride rescued me from having to recognize the truth.

To my surprise, as we waited for the signal, Nobody put her hand in mine. Just as Gretl waved, she whispered, "I am sorry. You don't speak German like a parrot."

22   At the Railroad Station

"Oh look!" Nobody was pointing.

I followed the direction of her finger, but could see nothing unusual. Before us was a large horse-chestnut tree.

"I thought they had all been locked up!" she exclaimed.

"What did you think had been locked up?" I asked in utter confusion.

"The trees." Nobody smiled; and then as she passed the tall, sprawling tree, which had not yet begun to bud, she bowed and bid it good-day. "It worried me, for where would the birds nest? But then I thought that they had probably put all the birds, except the crows and seagulls, in cages. But I see they haven't, and they left the sun in the sky, too . . . But I knew that because it used to shine in through the little window in the roof."

"It must have been strange," I said, glancing at my

companion, "to have to stay in such a small room for such a long time."

"The first month, Gretl locked my door. I don't know whether she was afraid someone might find me or I would try to get out. But later, she usually left it open. It is worse in the beginning because then you know that there is something outside. But after a while, all this—," Nobody made a wide sweep with both her arms —"is not real any longer. The only place that exists is your little room." The girl stood still. "You become like someone who is very old. You think of everything that has happened and never of what is going to happen."

"Do you think that's the way very old people are?" I asked as we began walking again.

"Yes," the girl replied. "You see, they know they are going to die." We had come to a corner. "We turn here," she said and suddenly smiled. "I remember walking along this street with my mother."

It was a broad avenue. We had left the alleys and lanes behind us. "I have never thought about being old," I said.

"That is because you are a very little boy," Nobody teased. "But you will grow old and then you will look like that man over there." Nobody motioned toward an elderly man on the opposite side of the street. He carried a cane and had a mustache like a walrus's, all yellow from tobacco smoke.

"If I am a very little boy than you are an even younger girl." I was looking around for some old hag that I could compare her to, but none was visible.

"No, I am not!" Nobody's voice quivered and I feared

that she was going to cry, "I will never be a young girl again!" Then, probably because she was near tears, she insisted that we walk faster: "We must hurry or we'll be late for the train."

The main railroad station in Hamburg is very large and almost always filled with people. We were early. The train for Kiel was not at the platform yet, so I went over to a stand and bought us frankfurters and rolls. Although they were different from the Danish ones, I thought they tasted good.

A boy a little younger than myself came up to us and asked whether I knew which platform the train for Lübeck was leaving from. He prefaced his request with a brisk *"Heil* Hitler!"

I had so completely forgotten the uniform I was wearing that I almost replied with some Danish absurdity, but I remembered just in time. As my right arm shot up in a fraternal hail to Adolf, I could feel my cheeks grow red.

"I liked you for blushing," Nobody said earnestly, after I had told the Hitler Youth the platform number, which by chance I had noticed when I was checking our own train.

"Everybody assemble here!" a loud voice boomed in Danish.

I might have jumped out of my black shorts, had I not had my shoulder strap on. The Lighthouse was standing about twenty meters away.

"Come," I whispered to Nobody, and grabbing her arm I pulled her along with me, while she popped the last bite of the frankfurter into her mouth.

"What's the matter?" she whispered as soon as we were hidden behind a newspaper stand.

"That was the Lighthouse," I said. "My teacher from Denmark. I forgot that this was the day they were leaving Hamburg. You can see them over there: a long pole surrounded by boys," I said and pointed.

"I like that they are not wearing uniforms," Nobody remarked quietly, as she stared at my comrades who were clustered around the Lighthouse.

"Some of them would not mind having them and neither would the teacher. He would love to be an *Übergauleiter.*" I spotted Nikolai. "Can you see the short fellow there with the suitcase in his hand?"

"Yes, he is funny-looking."

"That's the one!" A sudden inspiration made me say, "Go over and tell him that Erik wants to talk to him, but don't let anyone else hear you."

Nobody looked at me as though she were going to object; but just as I was about to tell her not to do it, she darted out from behind the newspaper stand.

I watched her. She only spoke to Nikolai for a second, and she made a grand circle before she returned to me.

"Did he say anything?" I asked. She laughed and nodded in the direction of the Danish boys. "Can't you see, he's already on his way."

I didn't know what I wanted to say to Nikolai. More than anything else, I probably wanted to brag, to tell him that I was smuggling a poor girl out of Germany, in the style of *The Three Musketeers.*

"Mein Gott!" Nikolai shook his head in amazement as he stared at me. "Where did you get that outfit from?

174

Or have they converted you and should I say *Heil?*"

"Don't be silly." I held out my hand toward the girl. "This is Niemand. We are taking the train north to Flensburg in a few minutes. We shall try and cross the Danish border tonight."

"Niemand!" Nikolai grinned. "But that means 'nobody' in German."

"Yes, and that's what she likes to be called. Her father was a Jew shot by the Nazis, and the Gestapo is after her." I reeled off these accomplishments, knowing that in Nikolai's eyes, they would enhance both the girl and myself. Almost with an air of boredom, I suggested, "When you are on board the ferry—but not before!—I want you to tell Stinker Larsen all about what happened to me."

"I can't." Nikolai was looking at Nobody, not at me. "Stinker is staying here in Hamburg to try and find you; and so, by the way, are the police."

I glanced around quickly, as if I expected a Gestapo officer to be lurking in the shadows ready to arrest me. "We've got to hurry. Will you telephone my father when you get back to Copenhagen?" I took out a pencil, but I had no paper.

Nikolai searched his pockets and finally found a wrapper from a chocolate bar, and I wrote my parents' telephone number on it. We shook hands very ceremoniously, while Nobody watched us with a puzzled expression. We had been speaking Danish and she had not understood anything we had said.

Nikolai wished her good-bye and bowed in a manner that would have earned him a compliment from a dancing-school teacher.

When Nobody and I had sat down, on either side of the window in an otherwise empty compartment of the train to Kiel, she remarked, "Nikolai is a very nice boy!"

"How do you know that?" I grumbled. "He could be a horrid boy, who beats his old mother on Sundays, for all you know."

"No, he is a good boy like you." Nobody grinned. "All Danes are good."

"If you asked his teachers, I think you would get a somewhat different description of Nikolai's character." I had taken out the package of food that Gretl had given me. There were four sandwiches, two for each of us.

"And what would the teacher have said about you?" Nobody was lifting one of the slices of bread to see what was between them. "Would he have said you were a good boy?"

"No, he would not; and I would have hated it, if he did! But Nikolai—" Suddenly the embarrassing thought that I might be jealous came to me, and the truth of it stopped me from saying anything more.

"But Nikolai?" The girl repeated my words, as the train started.

"Nikolai is my friend," I said.

There was a commotion as some latecomer jumped on the moving train.

"He is a very clever boy," I continued, while I heard the conductor cursing as he banged the door of the car shut. "I wish he were here now; he would be a great help to us," I added, bending over backwards to make amends for what I had intended to say against him.

176

"Hey!" The two sliding doors of our compartment were opened just wide enough to allow Nikolai's grinning face to appear. "I thought I'd better come along," he said. Looking at Nobody he asked, "May I come in?"

The girl glanced at me and when she saw the expression on my face, she laughed. "Do come in, I am sure you will be a great help to us!"

23   Bummelzug

"The trouble with the Nazis is that you can't take them seriously." Nikolai took a bite of the sandwich I had just offered him. With his mouth full of food, he continued, "It is all so stupid. But they won't last forever. The working class will overthrow them just as they threw out the Kaiser."

"Did the working class throw out the Kaiser?" I suspected that what Nikolai said was a simplification, but in history I had never managed to do any better than just scrape by, so I didn't dare disagree.

"That is what my father says." Nikolai grinned. "And my mother, too. And if you take my advice, you wouldn't argue with her." Nikolai nodded towards Nobody. "Was her father a Communist?"

"Why don't you ask her?" I replied. "It is not polite of us to be talking Danish, anyway." My German was much better than Nikolai's; but then, German and English were the only subjects I ever got decent grades in.

"No!" Nobody shook her head at Nikolai's question. "He was just a musician! He played the violin." The girl seemed to be trying to recollect something. "He played very beautifully," she finally added.

"But why did they kill him?" Nikolai persisted.

"I don't know." Nobody was looking out the window at the flat landscape. "They don't have to have reasons for what they do."

I was never sure whom Nobody meant when she said "they": the Nazis, the Gestapo, or some unnameable force of evil.

"They came at night," she said. "I remember I was in bed. They took my father away, and the next day we were told that he had been shot. Then Gretl came. Her husband had been shot, too."

"Gretl's husband had been in the S.A.," I explained. "It was in the Röhm Purge," I added smugly. "And after that Nobody had to live with Gretl in the *Keller*." I was about to go on and describe her miserable room in the attic when I noticed the girl looking at me as though she were angry.

"No, Erik, I lived with my mother for almost three years after that, just she and I alone. My mother said they shot my father because he was a Jew, but Gretl always says it was just a mistake, that that night they had made lots of mistakes. Funny, isn't it? I often think of those words: 'Just a mistake!'" Nobody stared straight ahead, as if she were contemplating them now. "But it was no mistake that they killed my Uncle Werner; and I am glad they did!" The girl glared at us as if she were

179

daring us to disagree with her. "Didn't Gretl herself say that he was bad? He would come and visit my mother when my father wasn't there. He called me *die Jüdin,* and would pinch me and pull my pigtails."

"Now you know, Nikolai," I muttered, "that you have to take them seriously."

"No, one shouldn't! One should always make fun of them! They don't deserve any better," Nikolai insisted. "Adolf is where he is because everyone took him seriously. He should have been laughed at, and then he couldn't have been made Chancellor of Germany!"

"Especially with a mustache like his," I said and grinned. "But all the same, we had better wait to laugh until we are back in Denmark." We were pulling into yet another whistle stop. "It halts at every station," I said.

Nobody was staring again through the glass. "Yes, I like that. It gives you more time to see things; and at every little village you can dream what it would be like to live there. I like traveling by *Bummelzug,*" Nobody said, as if she had forgotten the danger we were in.

I laughed, for the word for "milk train" in German, *Bummelzug,* was almost the same as the Danish and equally ridiculous.

"I know what you mean," I agreed. "Look!" I pointed to a bakery across the street from the station. "Imagine that you have looked a thousand times at all the cakes in that window. Sometimes you have bought some, but sometimes you have just looked. There are several stores like that on my way home from school; I look at them and I don't. I know every stone in their walls, and yet I no longer see them. Somebody knows that bakery in just

180

the same way, and every other house in that street." The train was moving once more. "I don't even know the name of the village."

"It is something with *dorf*," Nikolai remarked with annoyance.

'He is jealous, too,' I thought, and liked him the better for it.

"I wouldn't like to live in a village," Nikolai continued. "No, a city is better. There you can breathe freely."

'Funny,' I thought, 'that Nikolai should use the same expression I would have used to explain why I prefer to live in the country.'

"A city is best for hiding in." Nobody was very serious. "That is why Jews have to live in towns. They can't stay in the country because you can't hide there."

"But why should they have to hide?" I asked.

"They are always after them. Always! And in the city you can hide, though I would like to live in the country best of all."

"But there have not always been Nazis. In Denmark, Jews can live in the country if they want to," I said a little defensively.

"Oh, *they* have always been there. They just called themselves something else." Nobody sighed. "Oh look!" she exclaimed. "See the horses!" In a field a mare was grazing with a small colt, so young that it could hardly stand on its spindly legs. "In Dänemark, everything is different. There it rains soda water, and all the pigs are made of marzipan."

"That is not true! Denmark is a bourgeois capitalistic society, and Erik's father is a millionaire and he lives on

181

marzipan and never drinks anything but soda water, while the working class get only black bread and skimmed milk." Nikolai was laughing happily. It was the longest sentence he had yet ventured to say in German.

"And black bread and skimmed milk are much better for you," I replied; and then, I observed a little sourly in Danish, "There were four sandwiches. I had only one and Nobody had one. I wonder where the other two went."

"Into the very hungry belly of the proletariat. I didn't think about it; it was a case of absent-mindedness."

That wasn't true, because I had noticed Nikolai eyeing the last sandwich a long time before he took it; but I didn't want to argue about it.

If Nobody liked to travel by a slow train, she certainly was getting her chance with our *Bummelzug*. It seemed to me that it stopped not only at every station but at a half a dozen places in between. Finally, the conductor called out that Kiel was our next stop.

We were to take another milk train for Flensburg, which left in half an hour. No one in his right senses would travel to Denmark in this fashion; in that Gretl was correct. But now it suddenly occurred to me that she might have had another reason for sending us on this particular train. It would have given the police more than ample time to arrange for our arrival.

The train was slowing down and I was strapping my knapsack to my back. "Do you trust Gretl?" I asked Nobody.

The girl understood immediately what I meant and sadly shook her head. In the corner of the compartment there was a map of the district; I stood before it, studying it carefully.

The few travelers in the train had lined up in the corridor. We took our places in the back of the line.

"You go out first," I said to Nikolai. "If you see any police, make a sign and we will wait."

But it wasn't necessary for Nikolai to be our scout. As the train slowly made its way up to the platform, I saw Freiherr von Klein and two gentlemen in black uniforms. Like all persons of importance, we were being met by a welcoming committee.

24   The Shy Gestapo

The first of the passengers had opened the door and departed; the line was moving quickly. I looked out through the window of one of the doors to a compartment. There was no train on the track parallel to ours; beyond that was a deserted platform.

Turning to Nikolai, I said, "You take Nobody and go out of the door on the opposite side. You will have to jump down from the track, but the platform next to ours is empty. Get out of the station as fast as you can without attracting attention, and take the road to Eckernförde. I will catch up with you."

We were the last passengers. As soon as we were alone, I quickly unlocked and opened the door. The drop to the track was greater than I had expected, but Nikolai jumped without hesitation; and although he fell, he was up at once, ready to help Nobody.

When I finished locking the door, they were already

climbing the concrete wall to the platform. I waved, but neither of them saw me. Then I stepped out of the train and looked around as any normal passenger would.

The Freiherr spotted me immediately and called out my name. I turned towards him, while I debated whether I shouldn't just try to bluff my way out of the situation. After all, I was a Dane and a schoolboy; what could they do to me? But one of the black-clothed gentlemen with him started to run towards me, and I decided at least to give him a race before he arrested me.

There was a low fence separating the two gates that gave access from the platform to the station; since there were people passing through both of them, I decided to try to jump over the wall. As I have mentioned, athletics of any kind are not my strong point. The fence was about three feet high and normally I should have fallen flat on my face; but as it was, I put my hand on the railing and vaulted the fence in the style of a true gymnast.

The Gestapo officer, who like his boss Himmler had probably recently failed the test for the Athletic Proficiency Badge, did not have sufficient confidence to follow me. He chose one of the gates, where he collided with a middle-aged fat woman carrying an exceedingly full pair of shopping bags. I suppressed my inborn sense of chivalry and did not help her pick up the ten pounds of potatoes that were rolling along the pavement. Unfortunately, the Gestapo officer was not a gentleman either, and though I gained fifty meters at the outset, I feared he might quickly close the gap.

As I raced down the rather busy street, I realized the full advantage of a Hitler *Jugend* uniform—people either ignored me or got out of my way as if they thought I might be *der Führer*'s personal messenger. But never having been in Kiel before, I had no idea of the direction I was running in. Once or twice I glanced over my shoulder. Both of the Freiherr's friends were now following me, but the "nobleman" himself was nowhere to be seen.

My heart was beating fast and seemed to be moving further and further up towards my throat. 'I can't keep it up much longer,' I whispered to myself; but then I suddenly recalled that I had forgotten to give either Nobody or Nikolai any money, and I knew that my friend had spent the last of his on the ticket to Flensburg. This realization momentarily renewed my energy, for how were they to get along without a penny in their pockets?

My pursuers neither gained on me nor fell behind. No matter how many corners I turned, I could not shake them. As I dashed down yet another street, I read the sign, Eckernförderstrasse.

'At least, I am running in the right direction,' I thought. But it was as if this bit of a mental process were the final straw on the camel's back: I could not run any longer!

Breathing like a steam engine, I stopped in front of a restaurant-cum-beerhall, and entered together with a couple of thirsty men in overalls. The tavern was to the right, the restaurant to the left, and at the back of the entrance hall a stairway led to whatever the upstairs contained. A naval officer was mounting it; I climbed up behind him.

186

I reached the top of the stairs just as the two men in black uniforms entered the hall. Before me were three doors: one marked MEN, another LADIES, leaving little doubt as to what was behind them. The third might have led to something more useful to a fugitive, but it was locked.

The Gestapo officers had reached the foot of the stairs. The naval officer, who had been ahead of me, went into the men's room. In my hopeless situation, I was just about to do the same, when a sudden impulse made me open the door that said LADIES instead. There was no one in there; I left the door a little ajar so I could hear what was happening.

My pursuers also tried the unmarked door first. Outside the LADIES, they paused. I tried not to breathe, while I prayed most fervently that their mothers had brought them up to be shy.

Possibly because they had already had one unfortunate encounter with a lady, they chose to investigate first what was behind the door they had every right to enter. I waited a few seconds and then stuck my head out. The landing was empty.

On tiptoe I made my way to the stairs. I could hear strange goings-on coming from the men's room. One voice was bellowing "Open!" while another was cursing. I could not help feeling sorry for the poor naval lieutenant. Once you have seated yourself in one of those small compartments meant for privacy, the last thing you want are two Gestapo thugs rattling at your door and demanding that you unlock it "in the name of the law." I could not wait to give him my sympathy, however, as I had no urgent wish to meet his tormentors.

Once out in the street again I was about to start my athletic endeavors, when by chance I noticed a bicycle leaning up against the wall. It was unlocked, it was for a boy, and the saddle was just the right height for me. My conscience said, "Erik, that is stealing!" while I leapt onto it and rode away.

I kept looking back, but I had finally eluded the two men in black. No one was following me.

Near the outskirts of Kiel, I came upon Nikolai and Nobody. He was holding her hand, or rather, dragging her by the hand, for the girl seemed most reluctant to move.

"Nikolai!" I called, and they both turned around. Grinning, I jumped off the bicycle. In my mind I was already phrasing the story of my triumph over my enemies when Nobody's tear-stained face absorbed me. "What has happened?" I asked.

"She wanted to give herself up, for your sake." Nikolai snorted. "Damned silly girl . . . I had to drag her away. We saw you running with the Gestapo right behind you, so she wanted to give herself up!"

"I remembered that you had no money, so I could not let them catch me," I said gaily.

Nobody looked down at the ground, as if she had committed some kind of crime and was waiting for her punishment. I did not know what else to say, so I mumbled, "Thank you."

This made the poor girl blush. "I thought they might kill you," she whispered.

I was about to laugh and tell the girl that she was, indeed, very foolish; but then it occurred to me that if and when the Gestapo caught Nobody they would kill her. "Come," I said quietly. "We must get across the Kiel Canal as soon as possible. You sit on the crossbar, Nobody; and you, Nikolai, can hang onto the saddle and run beside us. When you get tired, we can exchange."

Twice Nikolai and I exchanged places before we reached the bridge over the Kiel Canal, which crosses Schleswig-Holstein to connect the shores of the Baltic with the North Sea. As we neared it, I kept looking to see whether Freiherr von Klein or his friends might have arrived there before us; there are not that many bridges over the canal. But the one we were approaching was not even guarded. It served as a crossing for the railroad as well as for ordinary traffic.

Once we were on the other side, we felt safer. For the first kilometer or so, the railroad tracks followed close to the road; when they parted, all of us agreed that it would be wiser not to continue on the main thoroughfare.

"I'll throw the bicycle into some bushes," I said. "I don't want anyone to find it for at least a day or two . . . It'll only be in our way, when we are walking alongside the train tracks."

"You see those trees in the field over there?" Nikolai pointed to two very tall elms. "Nobody and I will wait for you there."

I had just shoved the bicycle into a patch of briars when I heard a car coming. I threw myself to the ground.

They couldn't see me, but I could see them.

It was a black automobile moving as slowly as it could. In the front seat beside the driver sat Freiherr von Klein, scouring first one side of the road and then the other.

'He has a face like a fox,' I thought.

25   On the Road

It was the middle of the night when we passed through the town of Eckernförde. We were all so tired that we could have lain down on the tarmac and slept as soundly as if we had been lying in a feather bed.

Recalling my school atlas, I remembered that the sea makes a deep cut into the land at the town of Schleswig, which meant yet another bridge to cross. I thought that we ought to be on the other side of the fjord before sunrise, but it was not easy for me to persuade my companions to keep on walking. Before nightfall, we had found a store in a tiny village where we were able to buy salami, cheese, and bread. I had also purchased some chocolate, which I used as encouragement for my weary troops.

The sun was well above the horizon when we crossed the fjord, but our luck had not left us—the bridge was as unguarded as the one over the Kiel Canal. At noon, a wagon drew up from behind and its driver, a very stocky farmer, offered us a ride. He was returning from the creamery and he wanted company.

"You will have to admit—," my host looked at me sternly. I was sitting beside him on the wooden bench that was the driver's seat, while Nobody and Nikolai sprawled out on the boards between the aluminum milk cans. "You will admit," he began again, "that he has brought order and discipline." Obviously the farmer was continuing an argument that he had had with someone else. "Now I like to run my farm in a tidy manner. Discipline and order, I say, are the wheels of the wagon; without them you won't get very far."

Hastily, I agreed, for wheels on a wagon are a good thing, that is unless it is snowing, and then you want runners, in order to make it into a sleigh.

"Now I don't like back talk on my farm. Whatever I say goes. If I say that it is plowing weather, then we do the plowing. Can you blame *der Führer* for wanting the same? I say: *ein Volk, ein Reich, ein Führer* . . . One people, one country, one leader!"

I was about to suggest that maybe three leaders would be better, because they could work in eight-hour shifts, but somehow I didn't think that the man beside me shared my sense of humor. So I nodded vigorously, as I had before, which inspired him to shout, "*Führer befiehl, wir folgen!* Leader command, we follow!" I had seen both of these slogans painted on banners that stretched across the streets in Lübeck and Hamburg.

"How far is it to Flensburg?" I asked. I had had about enough of the philosophy of this tiller of the soil.

"You are not German!" The farmer sounded surprised,

192

which was quite understandable, considering the way I was dressed. "Where are you from?" he asked.

"I am Danish. I am here for the Easter vacation, and in Dänemark we are not allowed to wear the Hitler *Jugend* uniform," I explained.

"What a shame!" The farmer shook his head. "But the Danes have always been stupid . . . *immer dumm.*"

I turned around to glance at Nikolai and Nobody, who were following our conversation. At the words *immer dumm,* Nikolai stuck out his tongue, and I grimaced.

The farmer's thoughts, like a sluggish river moving ever in the same direction, had returned to his previous contention. "Without order chaos!" he declared; then, suddenly recalling my question, he added, "It is almost thirty kilometers to Flensburg."

I thanked him for the information without enthusiasm, for thirty kilometers would be far to walk, especially when we were so tired.

The farmer pulled on the reins of his horses. "This is the lane to my place," he said with pride, while pointing with his whip towards a small group of humble buildings.

The wagon stopped. I put my foot on the wheel and leapt down. Nobody was sitting on the tailboard ready to jump, and I held my hand out to her.

"Thank you for the ride," I said in German, while Nikolai shouted in Danish: "May your wife beat you, your dogs bite you, and your horse kick you before sundown!"

"*Heil* Hitler!" called the clodhopper as he touched the hind quarters of his horses with the whip.

"A regular kulak." Nikolai spat out after the departing farmer.

"What does that mean?" I asked. "I hope it is nothing pleasant."

"The rich farmers in Russia who were counterrevolutionaries were known as kulaks. Lenin starved them to death," Nikolai answered like a dictionary.

"It would take a while before you could starve him to death," I said, grinning, as I recalled the girth of the farmer.

"Do you know where we are going?" Nikolai asked as we wearily plodded along.

"I am not certain," I said, "but we are heading north and that will take us to the Flensburg fjord."

"They will be waiting for us at Flensburg, at the border," Nobody suddenly said. I looked with surprise at the girl, for her thoughts were uncomfortably close to my own.

"Why don't we steal a rowboat and cross the fjord?" Nikolai suggested.

"I wouldn't like to steal a boat," I said, although, as a matter of fact, I had been considering it, for it surely offered the best means of escape.

"Just say to yourself, 'I am borrowing it.'" Nikolai smiled.

"How far is it from the German side of the fjord to Dänemark?" Nobody asked.

"I don't know." I was trying to recall the contours of the land from my memory of the school atlas. "Three kilometers, maybe four. It depends where you cross it."

"I think we had better take a rowboat then," Nobody said most earnestly.

"You just can't take somebody else's boat," I said crossly.

"You took somebody else's bicycle," Nikolai chimed in triumphantly, "and even hid it in the bushes afterward."

"It was only a bicycle," I said evasively.

"It belonged to a poor boy whose mother had gone out early every morning to wash the floors of the rich; out of the pittance she earned, she bought that particular bicycle." Nikolai sniffed as though he were about to break into tears.

"Nonsense!" I exclaimed. "The boy who owned that bicycle was a Nazi. His father was an *Überuntermensch* named Pince-nez Heini."

"That's right!" Nikolai was laughing. "And we won't steal any boat. We shall, however, declare a revolution and confiscate private property."

"Once we are back in Denmark, I shall tell the police where we took the boat from and they will return it. I shall send whoever owned it money too," I added smugly.

"No, don't tell the police, or they might send me back with the boat." Nobody's voice quavered.

"The Danish police are not like that," I said and laughed. I was thinking of the jolly policeman whom I met almost every day on my way to school.

"Don't laugh." Nikolai was speaking Danish so the girl couldn't understand us. "My father was saying just before we left that he had read in the newspapers that our police have been sending refugees back across the border."

"I don't believe it," I replied; but I was lying, for I knew that what Nikolai said was true. I too had seen a photograph of the Danish police returning Jews who had come "illegally" into Denmark. I just didn't want it to be true.

The girl sighed and took my hand. "We can leave a note in the boat telling them where we have taken it from," I said.

Very quickly the boat that we had not yet stolen had become so much of a reality that I could see it in front of me.

"Have you ever rowed?" Nikolai asked. We were sitting in a ditch resting. It was almost noon and there was hardly any traffic on the narrow byway.

"I have rowed a boat . . ." I thought long and thoroughly and then admitted, "exactly twice."

"Which makes you twice as experienced as I am. Can you swim?"

"Yes, can't you?" I asked with surprise, as we were taught swimming in school.

"Not very well." Nikolai sighed. "My mother wouldn't let me take swimming lessons—she thinks it's bad for my ears. What about you?" he asked, turning to Nobody. "Can you swim or better yet, can you row?"

"I can't swim and I can't row, but you will teach me." Nobody looked at me appealingly.

"He can teach both of us." Nikolai got up. "I can't wait to get to that rowboat!"

26   The Punt

"That is Denmark," I exclaimed dramatically.

We had climbed a small hill, the only one in the land-scape. Below us, a few kilometers away, the waters of the Flensburg fjord glimmered, reflecting the light of the sun, which had just risen above the horizon.

"You mean over there?" Nobody stretched out her arm in the direction of the fjord and the coastline beyond it. "It doesn't look any different."

"Well, it hardly would," I said testily.

We had rested during the night, for a few hours, in a barn; but we had been so cold and miserable that finally all of us agreed that we preferred walking, even though we could hardly lift our feet.

"It *is* different, though." Nikolai rubbed his hands against each other. "Over there, we would walk into the nearest inn and order breakfast, then we would make Erik phone his rich father, who would come immediately

197

in his motorcar and take us home. Oh, it is different all right."

"I don't have any home he could take me to in his motorcar." Nobody shrugged her shoulders. "But the breakfast would be very nice." The girl looked at me. "What would you order?"

"Bacon and eggs and coffee," I answered and then, realizing how hungry I was, I added, "Toast and marmalade."

"Steak!" Nikolai shouted. "I don't care about breakfast, I want the dinner I didn't get last night."

"That is the trouble with Communists," I said and laughed. "They want all the dinners they have been cheated out of."

"That's right!" Nikolai was swinging his arms and slapping his back. "I keep an account of all the steaks I haven't eaten; as soon as the revolution comes, I am going to insist on getting them."

"Tomorow in Denmark, I shall buy you one," I said. "But let's go; we still have to find a boat . . . You know, there could be a baker in that village down there who will sell us some freshly baked rolls; in my opinion, they taste almost as good as steak."

"All right," Nikolai sighed. "At least, it is downhill. But there won't be any baker; the village is too small."

Nikolai was right. Not only was there no bakery, but the only grocer slept late. His shop was not open at seven o'clock in the morning.

On the beaches beyond the village, new disappointment awaited us. First of all, rowboats were not as plentiful as we had hoped they would be. Secondly, although people occasionally might leave their boats on the beach, they seldom supplied the oars and the oarlocks.

"They knew we were coming," Nikolai grumbled, as we discovered yet another boat drawn up on land minus mast, oars, and sail.

The water had hardly a ripple in the still April morning. "It doesn't look more than a couple of kilometers wide." I could feel the sun beginning to warm my back. "It's going to be a nice day," I said cheerfully.

"Erik!" Nobody called. She had gone ahead, and she had stopped and was waving her arms.

The stony beach ended in a clay embankment. There was a deep rift in it, and in this had been hidden something which a not too particular person might call a boat.

"Look!" Nobody held up a paddle. "There are two of them."

I kicked the side of the contraption. It was a punt, the kind that hunters use in the duck season. Its bottom was flat and had been tarred; its sides were no more than two feet in height. "I wonder whether it will float," I said uncertainly.

"Let's put it in the water and see if it leaks," Nikolai suggested.

We launched the tiny craft and waited. It didn't leak —at least, not very much.

Nikolai was all for starting out at once and we might have, had not a motorboat belonging to the German navy gone by, out in the fjord, just as we were preparing to embark. We decided it would be better to wait until evening and paddle across at dusk, when we were least likely to be noticed.

We returned the punt to the crevice in the embankment and concealed the paddles under it. Not far away was a small forest of pines; we found a clearing in it that made an excellent hiding place.

"I wish to God we dared light a fire." Nikolai was sitting on a tree stump.

"For God's sake, don't! You might as well climb the highest tree and say, 'Here we are!' "

"I don't even have any matches," Nikolai replied. "I just said I wished I could."

Nikolai sounded glum as well as irritated. Partly to placate him, I suggested, "I'll go and get us something to eat. Surely by now the store must be open."

"Shouldn't I be the one to go?" Nikolai asked.

"Don't worry, I'll be careful. Good-bye," I said, turning to Nobody who seemed lost in her own thoughts.

She smiled. "Hurry back," she said.

"Try and get a couple of bottles of milk," Nikolai called after me.

"A beautiful day!" The shopkeeper was all friendliness.

I nodded and smiled; I was determined to speak as little as possible, hoping that if I were silent, no one would suspect that I was not German.

A van had just delivered freshly baked bread and milk as well. By the time I had finished my shopping, all I had bought filled a big paper bag. As I was paying, I noticed a tray with Danish pastry on it. It looked almost as good as the real thing. I bought three pieces, which were given to me in a small white bag.

I had bid the man behind the counter good-bye and had started towards the entrance when the door opened. Blocking my way was Freiherr von Klein!

"Can I help you?" He took one step backward, and held the door for me. *"Bitte ..."* The German word for please sounded anything but pleasing.

I nodded as I passed him, and he closed the door behind us. "I am so glad to see you, Erik!" The Freiherr smiled as a cat might at a mouse caught in a corner.

"Where is the girl?" the Freiherr demanded.

"What girl?" I replied, trying not to look scared.

"Don't be stupid, Erik. We know you have the girl with you." The Freiherr held out his hand, as if he were pleading. "All we want is the girl. You give her to us and we will help you cross the border. You have nothing to worry about."

"And why do you want her?" While I was speaking I glanced around quickly for the two Gestapo officers who had been with him.

"It is our job to catch the fleas and then to ..." The Freiherr made a movement as if he were squashing an insect between his thumb and his forefinger. "She is what a true German finds more loathsome than a Jew." The Freiherr drew himself up, as if he were about to stand at attention. "The product of the criminal act of an Aryan fouling his blood and his race."

"It is her mother who is German," I could not help saying.

The Freiherr made a grimace which, I am sure, he

201

thought was a friendly smile. "I don't care, Erik. I am not a fool. What does it matter to me, what her mother is or her father was. I am not a prejudiced petty bourgeois! All that matters is whom her mother married! The girl is an embarrassment to him, so . . ." Freiherr von Klein snapped his fingers, while he breathed rather than spoke the last part of the sentence, "we must make sure she doesn't exist."

I was wondering whether the "we" referred to myself and the Freiherr, or to himself and the Gestapo, when it suddenly occurred to me that the Freiherr was trying to hold onto me with his tongue, because he feared that he couldn't with his hands until his friends in the black uniforms arrived.

"*Bitte,* hold this," I said quietly.

Just as I expected, the Freiherr responded to politeness and automatically held out his hands so I could put the big bag of groceries in them.

As I turned and ran, I shouted with glee, "You can keep them!"

27 The End

I glanced back. The Freiherr had been well brought up. Instead of throwing the bag of groceries on the ground and taking up the chase, he was carefully leaning it against the wall of the store.

But by the time I reached the wood in which Nikolai and Nobody were hiding, he was so close behind me that I could make out his features. Yet I stopped and called to my friends. I was not afraid of the Freiherr; the three of us would be more than a match for him, for I felt certain that he wasn't armed.

I could hear Nikolai come crashing through the trees. Freiherr von Klein was standing still less than fifty meters away. I bent down and picked up a stone.

"Don't be a fool, Erik!" he shouted.

I threw the stone and he took a few steps backwards, although it had come nowhere near him.

Nikolai was beside me. "We'll have to take the punt

and paddle across now," I said excitedly. "For he will sound the alarm, and then everyone will be out after us!"

"Why don't we kill him?" Nikolai asked most matter-of-factly; and then he threw a stone. Either he aimed better or he was luckier than I had been, for his grazed the Freiherr's shoulder and made him retreat still further.

"Because..." I was trying desperately to find some reason why we should not end the career of Freiherr von Klein. At last, because I could think of nothing else, I mumbled, "We are not like him."

"I should hope not, he is a fascist!"

Nikolai was busy picking up stones and throwing them. To my surprise Nobody had joined him, but hers fell far short.

It was then that I realized that I was still carrying the small paper bag containing the Danish pastry. "Here," I said, offering them each one.

Nikolai brushed his hands off on his trousers, and before accepting the cake, complained bitterly that his target had moved out of range. At a safe distance, the Freiherr was still standing watching us.

"Let him look," I said. "By the time he can get back to the village and find his friends, we'll be halfway across the fjord. Come on!"

Nikolai and I ran down to the punt, with Nobody following a little behind us. We carried the boat to the shore; she brought the paddles and a rusty old tin can that had been lying beside the punt, which I suspected might—though I hoped it wouldn't—come in handy.

As soon as we put the boat in the water, the Freiherr started racing towards the village.

'May he fall and break his neck,' I thought, as I helped Nobody into the boat. She sat down in the middle; Nikolai was in the bow.

Pushing the punt before me, I waded into the cold water of the fjord until it came above my knees, then I jumped into the stern. Our voyage almost ended in disaster before it had even got started, for I had not been aware that a flat-bottomed boat has to be treated with great delicacy. It is not very stable; when I jumped into the punt, I nearly capsized it.

"For God's sake!" Nikolai exclaimed, turning pale. "Remember neither Nobody nor I can swim!"

I grabbed a paddle and kneeling down I began to use it. In the bow Nikolai was paddling as well, and the punt was forging ahead. The art, we soon learned, was for the two of us to paddle at the same speed. If one applied more strength than the other then the punt would turn off course.

In the beginning, Nikolai set the pace and I had a hard time keeping up with him, but soon we settled down to a speed that suited both of us.

"The boat's leaking!" Nikolai cried.

I looked down. Because my feet were already wet, I hadn't felt it, but more than two inches of water were in the bottom of the punt. We had tested it without getting into it. Now our weight had caused it to lie so much lower that some cracks and splits, which we could not have known about, were below the water line.

Nobody took the rusty can and started bailing. The more water the boat took in, the heavier she would be to paddle—and the Danish shore still seemed very far away. My hope was that Nobody would be able to keep the water from rising, but soon it was apparent how futile that hope was. I began to fear that we would not reach the opposite side. I looked around. We were in the middle of the fjord; we could not even turn back.

Nikolai lifted a paddle high into the air. "We're in Danish waters!" he shouted.

"If you don't keep paddling, we'll drown in them!" I yelled.

Poor Nobody was getting tired, but she did not stop bailing. By now the punt was almost half-filled with water.

'Even if the boat sinks, there should be enough up-drift in her to keep the two of them afloat,' I thought. 'I could try and swim for the shore and call for help.'

"Look!" Nobody shouted.

A motorboat was bearing directly down upon us. It was the same one we had seen earlier, and I did not need to look to know what flag she carried!

"Keep bailing!" I screamed at Nobody; Nikolai and I paddled even harder.

"We are in Danish waters!" Nikolai shouted, although all three of us knew that whoever was on that naval craft probably didn't care which side of the border they were on, when there was no one but ourselves to see them transgress it.

It was but three hundred meters to the shore, but the drone of the motorboat grew louder and louder. Oh, it was bitter to be caught, when we had almost made our escape.

"Ahoy!" someone shouted from the other boat.

"Keep paddling!" I screamed, as much to myself as to Nikolai.

"Halt!" the voice commanded.

The little gunboat was lying still in the water; its motor was idling. I glanced back; the officer was beckoning us to return.

"They don't dare come any closer," I explained. "There isn't enough depth for their boat. But we must keep paddling!"

Our progress was very slow. Soon the water level inside the boat would be the same as it was outside. Nobody gave up bailing; there was no point in it. Little waves were breaking in over the sides.

The engine of the motorboat started again; she was turning, heading back for German waters.

"Hurrah!" shouted Nikolai, which seemed a little absurd as our vessel was sinking.

'I will swim and then the punt may carry them,' I thought heroically, as I let myself over the side into the cold waters of the fjord, expecting to have to battle for my life, for I was not a great swimmer.

The bottom was slimy mud. I was standing waist-deep in water. At the sight of me Nikolai started to laugh.

Nobody looked with surprise at him, then at me . . . And then . . . suddenly we were all three laughing so hard that it hurt.

Epilogue

We waded ashore. We were wet, dirty, and cold. But that didn't matter, we were safe. Later we found an inn, where Nikolai had his steak; and I phoned my father and, just as Nikolai predicted, he came in his motorcar to get us. But the story ends with us laughing in the cold water of the fjord.

An unhappy time was in store for Denmark. A few years later, it was invaded by the Nazis. I could not imagine that Nikolai would not fight them, could you?

Nobody had sailed to America quite a long time before that. Her uncle wasn't all that difficult to find; and like her father, he was a decent man.

And Erik? Oh, he was always a lucky boy. Every time he was about to drown, he found that his feet could touch the bottom. He was just a little spoiled and he still is, for although his hair is getting gray, he hasn't grown up yet, so I don't think he ever will.

I cannot even hazard a guess about what happened to the Freiherr or the poor midget; and about the former I don't even care. Unfortunately, people like Freiherr von Klein have an ability to survive.

What happened to the fifty Danish passports that probably cost the life of the man in the gray raincoat, whether any of them were ever of use to anyone or not, I shall never know, because that's the way it is in a real story, there are some things that you never find out.